I0687831

The Last Quarter

Nicki Edwards

Copyright 2021 Nicki Edwards
All rights reserved

Copyright © 2021 Nicki Edwards
All rights reserved.

DEDICATION

To a retired racehorse called Moderator ("Monty") who kept me
sane during 2020.
"No hour of life is wasted that is spent in the saddle."
(Winston Churchill)

Could this be her second chance at life and love?

Fiercely independent barrister Zara Pritchard never planned on returning to her hometown of Glengarrick, but a shock breast cancer diagnosis while pregnant with her son forces her to rely on others for a change.

For Dr Ryan Dunlop, Glengarrick is exactly the place he needs to avoid the spotlight after a simple mistake as an AFL club doctor almost cost him his career. As soon as the dust has settled, he intends to return to Queensland.

At least that's the plan until he falls hard for the first woman he meets in town. But Zara doesn't have time for romance. She's too busy with a new business venture and raising Finn, whose DNA she needs to keep a secret.

Can Ryan convince Zara he's the one for her and Finn? And if Zara opens her heart to Ryan, will his feelings for her change when he discovers the truth about her past?

Chapter One

Sideways rain lashed the windshield of Ryan Dunlop's Jeep as it roared over the grooves in the gravel road. He raked a hand through his hair as a single thought repeated itself over and over in his head. *Get to her. Get to her. Get to her.*

Lightning lit the night sky and, seconds later, thunder boomed. He gripped the steering wheel tighter and eased his foot off the accelerator. He couldn't help her if he ended up in a ditch. And it wasn't as though there were dozens of other doctors out here in the middle of nowhere.

Zara Pritchard was one of his clinic's patients but as the brand-new locum, he hadn't met her. According to the notes he'd pulled up on his laptop, Zara's labour was six weeks too early. And to complicate things, she had breast cancer.

Her friend, Georgina, had called half an hour earlier. Being a Saturday, the clinic was closed, but every second weekend he was rostered on duty and the phone got diverted to him after hours. Georgina had said his patient's contractions were three minutes apart and lasting a full minute. She'd been in labour since that morning but rather than head straight to the hospital, she'd stayed at home. And now it was too late to get to the hospital in Stockton in time. A hospital that offered comprehensive pain relief, and, more importantly, midwives.

Ryan forced his breathing to slow and beat back a surge of dark memories as he refocused his attention on the wet road in front of him. The one and only time he'd helped deliver a baby he hadn't been the attending doctor—he'd been the father. Not that he would admit *that* to a labouring patient.

Sheet lightning illuminated the sky again and he sent up a silent prayer there were no power outages. According to his GPS, the farm was close to a tiny dot on the map called Braxton. Barely big enough to be considered a town, Braxton boasted a well-appointed general store, which also served as the local post office and pharmacy, the CFA shed, and a primary school.

The nearest main town was Glengarrick where the clinic was, but it didn't have a hospital. Stockton did, but if Zara's contractions were as close together as Georgina said, there wasn't a hope she'd make it in time, even if he could convince her to leave. He dragged in a deep breath and exhaled in a rush. If he was about to deliver his first baby, at least he was doing it at someone's house rather than in their car on the side of the road. Especially with the storm raging the way it was. The wind had picked up and was buffeting his car.

Earlier in the day he'd been enjoying himself watching a local game of football in sunny Glengarrick. But towards the end of the last quarter the sun had disappeared, the heavens had opened, and it hadn't stopped raining since.

Despite his personal demons regarding a home birth, he had to step up and do what he'd been trained to do: ensure both mother and new baby made it out of this alive. With that in mind, he pushed his foot down on the accelerator again.

Five minutes later he arrived at his destination. Braxton Park. He slowed as he turned through the open gates and crossed a cattle grid. Seconds later the house came into view, lit with lights in every window.

Hauling his emergency doctor's bag from the boot of his car, Ryan bolted up the wooden veranda steps, heedless of the soaking rain. He knocked on the front door just as thunder cracked overhead.

No response.

He knocked again and when no-one answered, he turned the handle and let himself in. He called out, then stood in the dimly lit open plan living area, holding his breath, listening. The murmur of women's voices came from down a hallway. Adrenaline pumping, he headed in that direction, shoving down his anxiety. He had to get his emotions under control and keep a clear, level head. Just because the last birth he'd attended had ended in tragedy, it didn't mean this one would.

Ryan was a man who prized rationality, but he also had more than his share of professional pride. He could do this—and he *would* do this—because the mother and her soon-to-be-born baby depended on him. End of story.

Braced and ready, he knocked before opening the door. The bedroom was small but neat as a pin. Matching bedside tables and lit lamps were at either side of a queen-sized bed and what appeared to be a dozen pillows. His labouring patient was barefoot and wearing an oversized t-shirt. She paused her pacing over the carpeted floors and looked at him.

'Hi. I'm Ryan Dunlop. The locum GP.'

'Zara,' she managed, one hand at the small of her back, the other arm hooked around her friend's shoulders. 'And this is my best friend, Georgie. She called you.'

'Good to see you up and walking,' he said, dropping his medical bag on the floor. 'That'll help things along.'

'I found it the best thing to do when I had my baby,' Georgie said. The tremor in her voice was unmissable. She was terrified. 'I wasn't sure what else to do.'

Clearly he was going to get little help from the friend. It was going to be up to him.

'You know she's early?' Georgie continued. 'She's not due for another six weeks.'

He nodded, trying to focus on his medical expertise and not his racing heart.

'I probably should have called for an ambulance,' Georgie said with a frown.

'I'm fine,' Zara said, waving away her friend's concerns. 'Women have been doing this for…' She groaned and stopped walking as another spasm of pain gripped her abdomen.

'Is there a husband or partner?' Ryan asked. With the storm, there was every likelihood the father of Zara's baby was out on the farm checking livestock or fences or something instead of being here where he was needed.

'Single. Mother. No. Husband.' Each word came out through gritted teeth.

There was a story there, but now was certainly not the time.

He pushed aside his personal feelings and put on his professional mask. He took in the flush over Zara's cheekbones, the rapid throb of the pulse at the hollow of her throat, the way her bloodless lips moved silently to count out the seconds of the contraction. It was obvious she was in the final stages of labour.

He needed to examine her to be sure. The midwives at the hospital where he'd done his training always said not to intervene unless it was absolutely necessary. But he was in the middle of nowhere with no medical support, and he couldn't afford to leave anything to chance.

He stood and watched until the contraction eased, then moved to her side and gently nudged Georgie out of the way. Exhausted, Zara swayed on her feet and Ryan caught her elbows, supporting her weight as she fell back against his chest. She dropped her head back onto his shoulder and he froze as the memories swelled. The last time he'd held a labouring woman in his arms, things had ended badly for all concerned.

Shaking his head to rid it of his frustratingly persistent anxiety, Ryan glanced at Georgie standing in the doorway, clearly unsure what to do. She was pale and the last thing he needed was two patients. He needed to keep her occupied.

'Have you boiled the kettle?' he asked. 'And we'll need clean towels or sheets, a big stack. Also, if Zara has a tumble dryer, you can use it to warm some towels for the baby.'

Georgie straightened. 'I can do that.' She glanced at Zara. 'Are you okay if I leave you for a minute?'

Zara lifted a shaking hand to wipe her damp, blonde hair off her sweaty forehead. 'It's fine, George. Dr Delicious here will take care of me.'

Ryan bit back a smile. He'd been called a lot of things over the years, but Dr Delicious was a new one. He met Zara's eyes and in that brief moment of calm lucidity, a connection clicked into place. For the next little while, he and Zara would be a team, working together to bring a new life into the world.

After Georgie left, Zara transferred her weight to Ryan. Leaning on him, trusting him to hold her up as her next contraction built. She seemed only peripherally aware of him, her focus on managing her pain, but that didn't stop the surge of warmth that unfurled inside him. She had simply assumed he was up to the task, her trust a gift freely given. Now all he had to do was live up to her expectations of him.

'Do you want to lie down or keep walking?' he asked, his arms holding her steady when she wobbled again.

'What I *want*,' she said, grimacing, 'is to get this baby out of me.'

She panted for a moment, then looked up at him. For a moment he was struck by the liquid brown of her eyes, but the hint of fear in her gaze snapped him back into work mode. Swallowing, he fixed another smile on his face. 'You're doing an excellent job.'

'You can manage the delivery, right?' she asked, more wary than worried. 'And you're definitely a doctor, aren't you?' There was a brief flash of humour in her eyes before it disappeared, replaced by pain as another contraction surged.

He waited for it to ease, rubbing his hand over the small of her back. 'I don't think now's the time to give you a copy of my resume.'

'Fair enough. As long as you can handle a home birth. Let me assure you, it wasn't my plan.'

'Plenty of healthy babies have been delivered at home in far worse conditions than a clean, dry, warm, well-lit room. You'll be fine,' he said, as much to reassure her as himself. 'Is it okay if I examine you? I need to assess where we're at.'

She nodded and he rolled up his shirtsleeves and waited for her to make herself comfortable on the bed, settling back against a nest of pillows.

'I knew it was going to be painful, but not like this,' she said after a moment.

'Birth is the first clue we get that life is going to be messy and painful.'

She raised her eyebrows and he realised how cynical he must have sounded.

'The actual process of a baby entering the world usually isn't that complicated. They always know what to do,' he hurried on, hoping he sounded a little less pessimistic.

'Unless there are complications.'

Zara sounded calm, but her fingers clutching the quilt were white knuckled.

A thick weight pressed into his chest and he tried to swallow the lump in his throat. 'Then let's hope and pray for no complications.'

'I'm six weeks early.'

He wanted to tell her not to worry, that everything was going to be fine—but he wouldn't say that until after he'd examined her.

Zara lifted her t-shirt, and he shifted his gaze from her pale, strained face to the taut brown line down the centre of her swollen belly. His breath caught as old memories crowded in.

Zara wasn't Lisa. Wasn't his wife. She was his patient, and she was in pain. It took all his conscious effort to make the switch in his head.

Focus.

Chapter Two

The next twenty minutes passed in a blur. Working partly by instinct and partly by training, and letting Zara guide him, Ryan supervised her final stages of labour. Leaving the brow wiping and hand holding to Georgina, he maintained his position at the foot of the bed and tried to keep his mind on the job. To stay in the moment and not in the past.

He didn't intervene until the baby's head crowned.

Seconds later, with a hearty cry, a tiny scrap of humanity slipped out of Zara and into his hands. Zara's expression went from exhaustion to exhilaration in an instant.

Without a set of scales, Ryan had no idea what the little boy weighed, but he looked great, and his APGAR score was better than seven.

He quickly placed the naked squirming baby on Zara's chest and stepped back as Georgie put a warm blanket over them both. Plenty of time to deal with the cord later.

He kept his eyes down and checked Zara didn't need any stitches before cleaning up. He couldn't look at her face—seeing her look of relief had almost undone him. Rather than the agony he remembered on Lisa's face after the birth of their stillborn son, Zara's face shone with elation, the way it should. There was nothing about this birth that compared to the last one.

Ryan stood to the side and stared down at the wrinkled, red-faced baby clenching his tiny fists in rage and bewilderment at being suddenly thrust into the chilly air. His heart thrilled with every hearty scream that emerged from the baby's tiny lungs. He might be six weeks early, but he was perfect.

Without a word, Zara reached for his hand and he automatically took it. He sank onto the bed beside her and gazed down at her son. She rested her head against his chest and without thought he rested his chin on her head.

'Thank you,' she whispered, so quietly he wondered if he'd imagined it.

He squeezed her hand before releasing it and she slowly pulled away from him. He tried not to notice how empty and cold he felt, how the intimacy of the moment had felt like a balm to his wounds … or how attractive Zara was.

Stop it.

He slid off the bed and packed up his medical bag with shaking hands. What was wrong with him?

'He's perfect, Zara,' Georgie said, echoing his own thoughts as she stroked the baby's head. 'And he looks like you.'

'All ten fingers and toes.' Ryan barely recognised his own voice; it was so hoarse.

Another reedy cry jerked Ryan back into motion, and he dealt quickly with the umbilical cord.

What he'd told Zara was true. Birth was painful and messy. But when everything worked the way it had tonight, it was like touching pure joy. The experience of being with Zara for the birth was a pivotal moment for him. This child would always have a special place in his heart.

Ryan was so lost in his thoughts he missed Zara's question.

'Sorry? What did you say?' he asked.

'What's your middle name, Ryan?'

Ryan frowned. 'Why?'

'Well, it would be a bit weird to call him Ryan, but if I like your middle name, I might choose that.'

Ryan's lungs contracted as if he'd taken a hit to the solar plexus. He stared at Zara for a long moment before he realised he was holding his breath and she was waiting for his answer. 'I'm sure you have plenty of names picked out,' he managed to say.

He'd wanted to give their son his middle name, but Lisa hadn't really liked it. Then she was gone too quickly, and he never had the chance to ask her what she'd wanted to call their child. In the end he'd called the baby William, after Lisa's father.

'I haven't picked out any names,' Zara said with a shake of her head.

His thoughts bounced back to the present.

'I wanted to wait until I saw him first,' she said, 'and see what suited him.'

Ryan hesitated, but couldn't come up with any reason why he shouldn't tell Zara his middle name. If she didn't like it, it wasn't like she had to use it for her baby. 'Finnegan. My middle name is Finnegan.'

Zara tipped her head to one side before looking down at her son, resting against her chest. His cries had stopped, and his eyes were open, as if he were taking everything in and listening to them.

'Finnegan. I could shorten it to Finn. I like it.' Zara looked up at Georgina. 'What do you think, George?'

'It's up to you, but yeah, I like it. Finnegan Pritchard. It's strong.'

Unprepared for the emotions running riot inside him, Ryan turned away, so his face was hidden. Blindly rummaging through his medical bag and messing it up again, it took longer than it should have for him to regain his professional persona.

An unwelcome flare of hope burned in Ryan's chest. Why did he feel so connected to Zara and the baby? Yes, they'd shared a miraculous experience, and he was beyond relieved that both of his patients were flourishing but it was that moment of connection with Zara that had tapped into something he'd thought was carefully buried. Holding her hand, letting her head rest against his chest and standing over her as she'd held her baby, had cracked him open in a way that was both painful yet full of joy.

But he had no business feeling anything but professional concern for Zara and Finn. He was their doctor, and they were his patients. End of story. And professional ethics aside, he was only in Glengarrick for a month to fill in at the clinic. After that he was going back to Queensland where he had his dream job lined up as club doctor for the Gold Coast Suns. He'd been trying to get his foot in the door with the AFL for years and now he finally had his opportunity. The last thing he needed was the complication of a woman who lived in another state with someone else's baby. Especially a woman battling cancer.

Not that Zara looked unwell. Right now, her skin glowed and there was no evidence of her illness just by looking at her, but he'd read her notes and knew she had a large tumour in her breast. He felt sad for her, knowing she would have precious little time with her son before she began her treatment. He wanted to ask her about it, but this wasn't the right time. Knowing her diagnosis, he'd asked if she was planning to bottle feed and she'd vigorously shaken her head. She said she wanted to feed Finn, even if only for the first few days.

He stayed a bit longer to ensure mother and son were settled and Finn was able to feed. Satisfied with both of his patients, he picked up his bag and headed for the door.

'Thank you, Ryan,' Zara said, eyelids fluttering as she struggled to stay awake.

'You've said that already,' Ryan reminded her. 'About a dozen times.'

'I don't think I could have done it without you.'

He put down his bag and crossed back to her bed. 'You didn't need me at all. You did all the work. I was basically just the catcher.' It was a phrase he had picked up from the midwives at the hospital during his training and he'd always liked it.

Beneath the blanket that covered them, Finn made a snuffling sound against Zara's breast. He watched as Zara helped him find the nipple again. She winced slightly as he latched on.

'Does it hurt?' he asked.

'A little. It's a weird feeling.' She glanced up at him. 'It's probably best I don't feed him on the right breast isn't it?'

'It would be best to discuss that with your oncologist. He or she will have access to information that won't be on your file at the clinic.'

'To be sure, I might just stick to the one side.'

Georgie entered the room and sat on the bed next to Zara.

'Then you'll need to express from the other side,' Ryan said. 'The last thing you want is mastitis.'

Georgie nodded. 'You definitely don't want that. I have a pump at home. I'll bring it tomorrow. You can pump and dump.'

'Good idea,' he said.

For a minute no-one spoke. Then Georgie's phone rang, and she left the room to answer it.

Ryan watched Zara watching her son. Her eyes were hidden under a sweep of long lashes a shade or two darker than the spill of hair over her shoulders. When she blinked, tears fell, but she did nothing to stop them streaming down her cheeks.

His heart squeezed and he wanted to tell her she was going to be a great mum, but he didn't know that. He didn't know her story or her background other than what he'd read in her notes. He kept his lips closed. There was no guarantee Zara would be any better at parenting than anyone else. The only guarantee was that she'd mess up that kid the way all parents messed up their kids, even the loving parents. But if she could beat her cancer, she'd have the chance to try and get it right.

A familiar painful ache swelled and bloomed under his breastbone, like a spreader inserted between his ribs, cracking him open wide. He moved away from the bed and prepared to leave again.

Zara's voice stopped him. 'Are you okay with me naming him after you?'

He looked back at her and suddenly the pain in his chest eased. 'Very okay.'

As he left the room, the tears fell for another baby. A baby who should have had his name.

Chapter Three

As Zara watched Ryan Dunlop leave—she still couldn't believe she'd called him Dr Delicious—a funny sensation squeezed her heart. It almost felt like disappointment. For a moment she deliberated whether to call him back and ask him to stay with her a bit longer, but then common sense prevailed. He was her doctor, not her friend. Yes, he'd helped bring her son into the world, but what was a life-defining moment for her was presumably just another day in the office for him. Asking him to stay would have been strange.

The one person she should have been wishing to have with her was her best friend Ben, but everything about that felt odd too.

If she called Ben and Annabel they'd come straight out, but for now she wanted to be alone with Finn. Once her family and Ben found out the baby had arrived, they'd all want to visit and there'd be no peace.

She listened to the sound of Ryan's car leaving and another quiet shiver tingled down her spine. What a lovely man.

And thank goodness he was in town. Zara's usual GP had left at short notice for a family emergency two weeks earlier, promising to be back before Zara was due to give birth. Zara had heard a few whispers about the new locum doctor, but until tonight, she'd never laid eyes on him. All she knew about him was what she'd heard from the oldies in town. That he was aloof.

He hadn't been standoffish with her. Maybe he was just an introvert. Or shy. Or perhaps he was keeping to himself because he was only in town for the month and there was no point building lasting relationships with locals. But if tonight was an indication of the kind of doctor he was, he had a brilliant bedside manner. The man who'd let her squeeze the blood from his fingers during contractions had *plenty* of people skills.

It wasn't just Ryan's demeanour that had grabbed her attention though. His smooth voice had calmed and soothed her. It had stroked over her senses like a feather, filling her with confidence and helping her through every contraction.

Zara smiled. He'd ended up being better than Georgie who kept saying she was going to faint, which was hilarious, because she'd always said she wanted to be a nurse. In the end Ryan had banished Georgie from the bedroom saying he didn't need two patients.

It didn't hurt he was handsome enough that she'd felt a sizzle the moment he walked into her bedroom. And during her labour he'd been so kind and so patient with her that her attention had gone past his looks to who he was as a doctor…and as a man.

During labour, there had been long moments of silence between them, broken only by her moaning with each push. The entire scene had been oddly intimate, like a warm blanket cocooning the two of them away from the rest of the world. Even if he forgot about her, she would cherish the night and remember it forever.

She glanced down at Finn, now asleep between her breasts. She shifted him so she could look at him more closely. It didn't matter what Georgie had said. There was no denying who Finn looked like, and it wasn't her.

'How good looking is Dr Dunlop?' Georgie asked as she entered the room carrying a steaming bowl of soup. She placed it on the bedside table. 'I can't believe you called him Dr Delicious.' She giggled. 'You should have seen how red he went.'

Even at the mention of Ryan's name, Zara's heart beat a little faster, but maybe that was just the adrenaline leaving her body after the birth or the release of endorphins or something.

It was probably also because she was still feeling the emotional tug of the time they'd shared together, but right now Zara didn't want to get into a conversation with her best friend about Ryan's looks. Sure, he had a perfectly sculpted jaw, tousled brown hair, blue eyes and a broad, muscled back and shoulders, but objectifying him seemed somehow wrong. She had a feeling there was so much more to Ryan Dunlop than a pretty face.

Anyway, there was no point thinking about it. Nothing good could come from feeding her attraction to a man like Ryan. Especially when she had to focus all her attention on beating cancer. That, and Finn, were her only priorities.

At least she wasn't going to have to see him again. He'd be gone next week, and her regular GP would return. Which was just as well. It might be embarrassing bumping into Ryan in the supermarket knowing he'd seen all her 'bits'.

'Did you just whip that up now?' Zara asked, changing the subject to avoid answering Georgie's comment. 'It smells great. Thanks, George. Once I've finished this, I'll make some phone calls.' Her parents first, then, once Georgie had gone, she'd call Ben.

'I work in a café. I can make pumpkin soup with my eyes closed. Do you want me to take Finn while you eat?'

'I suppose I should give him a bath or get him dressed or something. What else do you do with a newborn?' She chuckled. 'I'd planned to read that book you told me about, but I thought I had a few more weeks up my sleeve.'

'I'll put a nappy on him for you and get him dressed unless you want to do that yourself.'

'Does it make me a bad mother already that what I want right now is food?' She shifted position in the bed and stared up at her friend.

'Not at all.' Georgie carefully took Finn from her and stroked his cheek with her pinkie.

Zara reached for the bowl of soup, took a mouthful, and swallowed. 'What time is it?'

'Just after seven.'

'Is that all? It feels like midnight.'

'The storm rolled in around four and got pretty dark.'

'Is it still raining?'

'Spitting.'

Zara took another mouthful of soup and moaned in appreciation. 'This is so good.'

'He seems lovely.'

'Who?' Zara asked. 'Finn? Of course, he's lovely.'

Georgie rolled her eyes. 'Dr Dunlop.'

'Yes, he seems lovely,' Zara agreed. 'A good doctor.'

'You'll need to go and see him for a check-up, won't you?'

Zara shook her head. 'Doubt it. Laura will be back next week. She'll be so ticked she wasn't here for the birth.'

'Has Laura said how long you have to wait before you can start treatment?' Georgie asked softly, concern in her eyes.

Zara blew out a steadying breath. Georgie had been tiptoeing around this conversation for weeks. 'She said about a week. I have to go to Melbourne for additional scans then I'll know more.'

'What did you decide about having the double mastectomy?' Georgie asked gently.

Zara loved her best friend, but she didn't want to have this conversation now. She wanted to enjoy her post-birth bubble and pretend everything was right in the world. As it was, she was having a hard enough time figuring out how she was going to raise a baby as a single mum, let alone facing her cancer diagnosis and treatment. Thank God Ben and Annabel and her parents had said they'd do whatever it took.

The last conversation with her oncologist had really rocked her when she'd advised Zara to have a total mastectomy. She hadn't thought she could cope with losing her breasts—she'd always thought of them as her best assets. But now, looking over at Finn, cocooned in a pale blue baby blanket, she'd gladly have her breasts removed if it meant saving her life and being there for Finn.

'I still haven't decided. It will all depend on what they recommend.'

'You're going to be okay, Zara,' Georgie said, tears pooling in her eyes.

A lump formed in the back of Zara's throat. 'I know I am.'

I'm so lucky, she reminded herself. Rather than wallowing in the "what ifs" she should be thanking her lucky, lucky stars with every breath and every beat of her heart. She had a community of friends and family who loved her dearly, and now she had the most beautiful baby in the world.

After a shower that lasted so long the hot water ran out, Zara returned to her bedroom to find Georgie asleep in the rocking chair with her feet on the footstall. Finn was also asleep, on his back in the bassinet at the foot of Zara's bed. The only part of him that was visible was his little head, covered in blonde, downy fluff.

Zara went to him and stroked his head, her touch super soft. He stirred but didn't wake. His head was still slightly misshapen, but his face, which had been red and blotchy when he was born, had taken on a perfect alabaster tone. His little lips were bright red, and they formed a perfect bow. He was gorgeous and she was in love. She gently scooped him out of the bassinet and climbed into bed, slipping under the covers, and sinking back into her pillows. While Zara had been in the shower, Georgie had cleaned up and put fresh sheets on the bed.

It was pitch black outside and the three of them could have been the only people in the world.

She ran her hand over her still swollen but now jelly-like belly. It felt so strange. She'd loved being pregnant and had focused all her energy on enjoying every moment rather than focusing on the cancer also growing inside her. The oncologist had warned her there was every likelihood she wouldn't be able to have another child, so she'd made the most of her pregnancy by wearing tops that showed off her glorious baby bump. She'd surprised herself that she hadn't been one of those pregnant women who didn't like to be touched. In fact, she never complained when locals approached her to pat her stomach and ask how she was doing or tried to guess the sex of the baby. When she'd hit the halfway mark, she'd renovated the spare room, painting it a pale lemony-yellow. She'd assembled the white cot and filled the drawers with everything her baby would need. And she'd had a car seat professionally installed, just to be safe. Even though cancer had loomed large, she'd had a sense of peace throughout her entire pregnancy.

For the next hour while Georgie slept, Zara cradled Finn in her arms, familiarising herself with every hair on his head. Even though she was exhausted, she was too tightly wound to sleep.

For a moment, their uncertain future loomed large, and a sense of panic threatened to overwhelm her. But she pushed the doubts away. Fear was normal. And her faith that she could beat this insidious disease was strong. Hugely strong. Even stronger than her fear. She looked down at Finn and kissed the top of his head.

It had to be.

Chapter Four

Two Years Later

Dawn. Zara's favourite time of day.

She crossed the yard, taking a moment to appreciate the band of tangerine streaking across the inky horizon. The promise of a new day and the start of a new week. The gradually rising sun would soon cast a golden glow over the paddocks, but there was a heaviness to the early morning stillness. And it was so cold her nostrils felt like they were glued together. She tugged her beanie over her ears and pushed her gloved hands deeper into her puffer jacket. It was freezing, but she loved these frosty Victorian mornings that hinted of snow.

Light spilled from the shed and, as she slid open the door and entered, she inhaled deeply, filling her nose with the scent of horses and hay. Instant warmth.

She still couldn't believe her luck, finding this property two and a half years ago and having enough money to buy it. The impressively named Braxton Park was in fact a tiny, recently renovated farmhouse. The big plus for Zara were the four shearer's cottages that came with the property, which she was able to rent out on Airbnb as farm stays. She also earned extra income by offering her paddocks for agistment. It was light years away from her former work as a barrister back in Melbourne, but even before her cancer treatment, she'd lost her courtroom mojo. Quitting her job and returning to Glengarrick to have Finn were the best decisions she'd made. Buying the property and running the accommodation was her third best decision. It meant she was able to stay at home full time to care for Finn. And her legal degree hadn't gone to waste. It had held her in good stead for starting and running her own business, especially when it had come to dealing with local councils.

A chorus of whinnies and the stomp of hooves on concrete welcomed her and she smiled.

'Morning boys and girls.'

Her cheery greeting inspired another singsong of neighs and she chuckled. The horses weren't happy to see her—they were hungry. She ducked into the feed room, noting the clock on the feed room wall read ten to seven. Finn didn't usually wake until seven thirty, so she had plenty of time before he came looking for her.

A radio probably older than she was hung in the doorway and she flicked it on. It was set to a station that only played eighties music and as she scooped out chaff and grain into buckets, she found herself humming to a familiar song.

Moments later she heard footsteps and stuck her head out, knowing who it would be without needing to look. Emily, one of the young women who stabled her horse here, often came out to feed and take off rugs even though Zara offered to do that as part of her fees.

'Morning, Zara,' Emily called out cheerfully.

'Morning, Em.' She passed Emily the bucket of feed she'd finished mixing. 'Are you riding this morning?'

Emily shook her head. 'Not this morning. It's too cold. And I have work today. But the forecast is for great weather all weekend, so I'll be back early Saturday morning.'

Zara's phone beeped and she pulled it from her pocket to read the notification. An email requesting a booking for this weekend. Short notice, but she'd had a late cancellation for all four of the cottages during the week so she could easily accommodate up to a dozen people if needed.

'Have a great day, Emily. I'll see you on Saturday.' Zara waved to Emily and headed back to the main house. With any luck she could make the booking arrangements before Finn woke.

She pushed open the gate in the fence that surrounded her house and gazed lovingly at the little farmhouse in front of her.

Her heart swelled with pride. She had done it. When she'd taken on the property, she'd known it would be a hard slog to make it work. Somehow in between her cancer treatment and caring for Finn, she'd managed to renovate the house and the cottages. She'd had lots of sleepless nights and every day a new challenge had greeted her, but she'd never once questioned if she was doing the right thing.

The real estate agent had listed the farmhouse as a 'renovator's delight'. That had been an optimistic depiction of the ramshackle home. The outside stonework had been crumbling, the paint on the window frames was peeling, the tin roof had needed replacing, and the veranda had been missing two posts. The yard that surrounded the farmhouse couldn't have been described as a garden. It had consisted of shoulder-high weeds but now, it was an oasis. She even had veggies growing.

She stepped over the crazy pavers set in the grass, jogged up the back steps and pushed open the back door that led directly into her light-filled kitchen.

Luck was on her side. Finn was still sound asleep in his bed when she checked on him. She was so fortunate her son loved his sleep. Probably because he exhausted himself during the day, only having the occasional day time nap.

She opened her laptop and pulled up the email. The booking was for a group of four men who wanted to get away from the city for a weekend-long buck's party. She pressed her fingers to her temples. The last group of men had trashed one of the cottages. But she needed the money, and it was bad business to turn down bookings. The fact they'd asked for two cottages was slightly odd—the larger of the cottages could easily sleep all four men— but it meant more money for her, so she wasn't about to complain.

She read over the overly chatty email again. Hamish, the groom, said they were looking for a chance to get away from it all. He sounded like a reasonable guy and she'd checked his references and he had good ratings on the accommodation website. She glanced out the window and smiled again as the sky changed colour. If a country escape was what these guys were looking for, they'd come to the right place. It wasn't like there was much for them to do this far out of town and no taxi or uber service to drive them home after a night at the pub. She confirmed their booking and closed the lid of her laptop as Finn made an appearance in the kitchen, wiping sleep from his eyes and demanding breakfast. Her morning moment of solitude had just ended. Not that she would have it any other way.

Chapter Five

Around five o'clock that afternoon, with Finn by her side, Zara let herself into one of the cottages for a final check. Her mother had been out that morning to make sure the two cottages were ready for their weekend guests, but Zara always liked to be sure Mum hadn't missed anything. She looked around with a sense of satisfaction. The bedding was neat, the pillows fluffed and there were fresh towels and locally made lemon myrtle soap in the bathroom. On the kitchen bench was a welcome basket with a bottle of local wine, fruit, and a loaf of seeded sour dough from the local bakery in Glengarrick and a package of handmade Anzac biscuits. In the fridge was a bottle of wine and another basket with a selection of cheeses, cured meats and dips, all locally sourced.

As she closed the door behind her, a wave of pride washed over her. The shearer's cottages at Braxton Park were charming and welcoming. Much better than staying in a room at the local pub—although she didn't say that out loud, given her parents owned the pub. Staying here was a unique experience where guests had the opportunity to get back to nature on a farm, nestled in Victoria's beautiful high-country.

From her property they could go horse riding or bush walking, and the local river was perfect for swimming in summer. For those who enjoyed fishing, it was full of fish. It was only a short drive to the ski fields too, so her business didn't slow down in winter.

She was heading to the second cottage when she heard a low rumble. She looked up and saw a cloud of dust that signalled someone coming down the long driveway. Both Emily and Morgan, the two girls who kept their horses at Braxton Park, had come and gone. Had Mum forgotten something when she was out earlier?

She watched a dirty white Grand Jeep Cherokee come to a stop in front of her house and she frowned, not recognising the car. The driver's side door opened, and a tall, broad-shouldered man stepped out in a pair of dark denim jeans and a blue and white checked shirt. He hadn't spotted her and Finn yet, so she had a moment to check him out. From this angle she couldn't see his face, but she could see he had a thick beard. Surely, he wasn't one of the guests arriving a day early, was he? She scooped Finn onto her hip and strode towards him, calling out a cheerful greeting.

He turned and smiled revealing white, straight teeth through the scraggle of his thick beard. 'Hi, Zara.'

She stopped and searched his face, meeting bright blue eyes. 'I'm sorry, have we met?'

His smile wavered. 'Didn't your mum call?'

She shifted Finn to her other hip. 'No.'

The man shoved his hands into the pockets of his jeans and rocked back on the heels of his boots. 'You don't remember me, do you?'

Finn fidgeted and struggled to be put down, but she held him tight. He was far too heavy, but she knew Finn, and if she let him go, he'd be making friends with this good-looking stranger in a heartbeat.

'I'm sorry, I don't,' she said, ransacking her mind for any memory of this man. Something about his voice was vaguely familiar but she couldn't place him.

'And this must be little Finnegan.'

Her pulse quickened. How did he know her son's full name? No-one called him that. He was always Finn.

The man's broad smile returned. 'Perhaps if I introduced myself as Dr Delicious you might remember me.'

Her breath locked and she looked him up and down again, mentally shaving off his beard and cutting his hair short. 'Ryan?'

He nodded and smiled again and in an instant the tension in her shoulders evaporated. She set Finn on the ground and strode towards him, arms outstretched.

'Wow. I didn't recognise you. Bit different from the clean-cut doctor I remember.'

After returning her quick hug, Ryan stepped back and ran his hands through his hair and down his beard. 'Yeah, I'm due for a trim.'

She chuckled. 'If you're going for the Ned Kelly look, I'd say you've nailed it. I have clippers in the shed if you want to borrow them.'

He laughed. 'No thanks. Might leave that to the professionals.' His gaze flicked over her. 'It's good to see you again. You're looking well.'

'I'm looking better than last time you saw me.' Heat swept up her neck. 'I'm surprised you recognised me. At least with clothes on.'

'I'd never forget a face that pretty.'

This time the heat in her face was from pleasure, not embarrassment. 'What are you doing here?' she asked, searching for neutral territory, and willing her pulse to normalise.

'You were right the first time. I'm actually one of the guests for the buck's party. I'm the best man. I got into Glengarrick earlier than I expected and I went to the pub to see if they had any accommodation for the night. Got chatting to a lovely woman. Turns out it was your mum. I should have realised. She looks just like you. I told her I was here for the weekend and staying at Braxton Park. I couldn't believe it when she told me you owned the place. She said you probably wouldn't mind if I stayed here tonight instead of at the pub.'

She glanced behind her then back to Ryan. 'Well, I suppose you can, but I still haven't finished checking the cottages are ready. I wasn't expecting your group until six o'clock tomorrow night.'

Ryan's brows drew together. 'Your mum said she was going to call you to check it was okay. I'm sorry, I assumed she had.'

Zara pulled her phone from her pocket. The battery was flat. She held up the black screen and showed Ryan. 'I'm sure Mum *did* call. I am shocking at remembering to charge my phone.'

'Honestly, if it's a problem, I can drive back into Glengarrick and stay at the pub.' His gaze moved from her to the sun setting over the green paddocks. 'Although this is far nicer than the room your mum offered me.'

She chuckled. 'Don't let my parents hear you say that. They think the pub is five-star accommodation.'

He chuckled. 'So, is this place yours?'

She nodded. 'Come on inside. It's freezing out and I need to get Finn his dinner. I can fill you in.' She turned to Finn who was splashing in a muddy puddle. 'Come on buddy, let's get you cleaned up.' She headed towards the house and stopped when she realised Ryan wasn't following her. She turned to face him.

He had his car keys out. 'I don't want to impose on you and your family, Zara. Honestly, if you don't want me to stay tonight, just say so and I'll head back into town.'

'Don't be silly. Finn and I aren't sending you away.'

'I'm happy to pay for an extra night though,' he added.

'It's fine. No big deal. It's just one night extra.' She opened the back door. Come on in.'

Finn tried to slip past her, but she tackled him and pulled off his filthy boots before shooing him inside. After slipping off her own boots she waited for Ryan to remove his then stepped ahead of him into the warm house.

'This is gorgeous,' he said, looking around. 'Like something from a magazine.'

Zara smiled. 'It's tiny but it's my favourite room in the house.'

The kitchen was warm and welcoming, and the centrepiece was an island bench with stools that invited guests to take a seat and enjoy a cup of tea. Large windows opened over the kitchen sink and the modern stove was set against the original bricks of the old fireplace. A cowhide rug on the polished timber floors finished off the country kitchen look.

She flicked on the kettle and set about heating Finn's dinner.

'Have you eaten?'

'Yeah, I have. Your mum said I had to have one of her famous chicken parmis.'

Zara chuckled. 'Famous. Mum cracks me up. They're not that good.'

'I beg to differ.'

The microwave beeped and she scooped Finn up and put him in highchair. 'Dinner's ready.'

'He's a cute kid.'

Zara smiled. 'He's the best.' She put a bib around his neck and placed a bowl of food in front of him.

'Are you going to eat too? Don't let me stop you.'

'I'll eat after Finn is in bed.' The kettle finished boiling. 'Can I make you a cup of tea? Coffee?'

'Tea would be great thanks. Just black.'

While she made their cups of tea, she watched him. He pulled out the stool closest to Finn and sat facing him, chatting to him and encouraging him with his food. 'He's a good eater.'

'Unless it's green.' She pulled out the stool next to Ryan and sat. She was generally a private person these days, so the warm and fuzzy feelings going through her watching Ryan engage with Finn surprised her. She gave herself a mental shake. Time to get back onto neutral ground. 'Do you know why the groom chose Braxton Park for his buck's party?'

'He didn't.'

She frowned. 'What do you mean?'

'I did. Apparently, that's the job for the best man. Hamish originally wanted to stay in an apartment in the city, but when I suggested a weekend of boating, camping and—'

'—fishing,' she finished for him with a chuckle. 'Well, you've come to the right place.'

'I know. That's why I suggested it.'

'Finn has just turned two. Have you ever been back here in that time?'

'No.'

'Well, nothing much has changed. You would have seen that when you drove in.'

'It's just as I remembered, only better.'

'Colder?'

'Yeah, definitely. I was here in spring and I remember being told you sometimes get snow.'

'We do. And if you're lucky, we might get some this weekend. It's forecast on the mountains and sometimes we get a light dusting that stays on the ground for a while.'

'So, how are you, Zara?'

She blew on her hot tea before replying. 'I'm great.'

'The cancer?'

She appreciated he didn't beat around the bush. So many people had tiptoed around her breast cancer diagnosis, not wanting to upset her. She didn't usually discuss her cancer with anyone, but given he was a doctor, it felt normal to tell him.

'Double mastectomy. Radiation. Chemo. They got it all. I have a clean bill of health. I have six monthly checks with my oncologist, but so far, so good. I'll relax when I hit the five-year mark.'

His smile broadened. 'That's brilliant news, Zara. I can't imagine the treatment was easy. Did you go to Melbourne for it?'

She nodded.

'Did Finn's dad help you out?'

His question sounded innocent enough, but was he angling for information?

'Finn's father isn't in the picture,' she said easily. 'Never has been, and we're okay with that.'

Ryan didn't comment or ask any more questions. He just took a sip of his tea and her estimation of him increased.

Only a handful of people knew Ben Mitchell, her best friend, was her sperm donor, and they both intended to keep it that way. She was fortunate that Ben, and his partner Annabel, supported her decision to raise Finn alone. While she'd had her treatment, they'd helped look after him, along with her parents and sisters, but none of them referred to Ben as Finn's father, because he wasn't, not in anything but the biological sense. When Finn was old enough to understand, they'd explain it to him, but until then, it was a tightly held secret.

Once her treatment was over, Zara was grateful for everyone's help, but she was keen to show them she could do it alone. Especially after Ben admitted they'd been trying for a family of their own for the past year with no luck. When Annabel offered to look after Finn one day a week for Zara, she graciously accepted her kind offer. So now, every Friday, Zara had some space and "me" time and Finn had a male role model. It worked well for everyone, although Zara wasn't sure how much longer those arrangements would hold. Last week Annabel had excitedly announced her pregnancy after six exhaustive rounds of IVF.

Finn finished his food and started smearing his hands through the mess on the tray of his highchair. Zara grabbed a packet of wipes from the benchtop and went over to clean him up.

'Ryan, if I give you a key, can you make yourself at home? You can choose cottage number one or two. They're the two furthest away from the house. You're welcome to light the fire, but I suggest you just turn the split system on—it will heat up the whole cottage quickly.'

Ryan stood and took their mugs to the sink. He rinsed them and left them to drain on the bench. 'As long as you don't mind.'

Zara lifted Finn from his highchair and slung him on her hip. 'Well, I'd prefer to have it ready for you and take you there myself, but it's late and Finn needs to have his bath and go to bed. And I still have things to do to get ready for the rest of your group tomorrow.' She went to a small alcove beside the kitchen that she used as an office and pulled two keys from hooks on the wall. She handed them over. 'Cottage two is my favourite. You'll get the best views of the sunrise over the valley in the morning.'

'Thanks, Zara.'

'You're welcome.'

She led the way to the back door and opened it. 'There are sensor lights on the shearing shed so when you drive past it, you'll easily spot the cottages as you drive down the hill.' She smiled. 'I'll see you in the morning.'

Ryan slipped past her into the cold and she followed him out, closing the door to keep the heat in.

He pulled on his boots, then hesitated. 'It's really good to see you again Zara.'

Suddenly his arms were around her again. She stiffened for a second before allowing herself to relax in his arms. It was just a friendly, warm hug, nothing more, and it felt nice.

He let her go, then jogged to his car, stopping to wave before she opened the door and went inside, closing it behind her.

She wasn't always quick to pick up on flirting, but there'd definitely been appreciation in his gaze. And she'd admired him too. Ogling him for a little longer than was probably appropriate.

For the next hour she was too busy to think about Ryan as she bathed Finn, read him two stories, and tidied up the usual mess in the kitchen and living room. By the time the house was neat and tidy the way she liked it, she put her own meal—a lasagne Georgie had made earlier in the week—into the microwave.

While it was heating, she stood at the kitchen window and stared out into the dark towards the cottages wondering which cottage Ryan had chosen. From this angle she couldn't see any lights. What was he doing inside? Hopefully he'd lit the fire and was relaxing. Or perhaps he'd filled the deep bath and was soaking in it. The last image lingered in her mind a fraction too long and she blushed. Closing the kitchen blind, she took her dinner out of the microwave. She would gain nothing picturing Ryan Dunlop in the bath. Or shower, for that matter.

Still, she couldn't deny the way her stomach tightened or ignore the funny flutter in her chest.

Chapter Six

Ryan climbed back in his car and followed Zara's directions past the shearing shed and down into a valley. He crossed a small creek and drove straight past cottage one, not bothering to stop to check it out. If Zara said cottage number two was the best, he'd take her recommendation.

He felt a stab of guilt he hadn't told her the real reason he was back in town, but in truth, he was surprised she hadn't heard. He'd assumed it would be local knowledge that the current GP was taking maternity leave, and that Ryan was her replacement for twelve months.

Or maybe Zara *did* know, wasn't happy about it and had simply acted surprised to see him.

Anyone who followed the AFL would know why he needed a new job. And there were plenty of people who still thought he was guilty even though he'd been cleared of any charges. Mud had a nasty habit of sticking.

Not only had he lost the job he loved, had his name and reputation as a doctor tarnished, but when he'd split with his girlfriend, Malinda, he'd lost a lot of his friends too. To protect Malinda, he'd signed a confidentiality agreement and couldn't give anyone the details of what she'd done until after the court case. A court case that might be years away. The club had publicly exonerated him, but it seemed he was still on trial by social media. The story would die down for weeks, then something would happen, and it would flare up again.

He shoved the negative thoughts aside as he pulled up outside the second cottage, a sensor light coming on and illuminating a large, grassed area around the cottage. Grabbing his bags from the back of his Jeep, he took the steps to the front door two at a time.

The cottage was perfect. He chose the smaller of the two bedrooms, pulled out his toiletry bag and unpacked his clothes, knowing Hamish would want the larger one with the small ensuite.

What he also hadn't told Zara was he'd been driving for sixteen hours and was exhausted. He'd planned to break the trip into two days, but in the end, he'd pushed through and driven straight through, which was why he'd arrived a day earlier than Hamish and the other guys.

His plan was to spend the weekend at Braxton Park, then search for somewhere to live on Monday. The current GP had decided to stay in town after she had her baby, which was a shame because her house would have been perfect. It was located right next door to the clinic and Ryan would have happily rented it from her. He'd searched for rentals online but there didn't appear to be anything other than short stay holidays rentals. Hopefully, if he asked around, the locals would put him onto something.

As he set about making a fire in the large wood-burning heater, he smiled when he thought about Zara's reaction to seeing him again. First wariness—and he felt bad that he'd frightened her by showing up out of the blue—then surprise had flickered in her gaze, which quickly became delight.

He had only thought about Zara from time to time over the past two years. It was funny how she'd sneak into his thoughts at odd moments. But it wasn't until he was searching for GP jobs and the one in Glengarrick popped up that he realised his heart had beat a little faster when he thought about the possibility of seeing her again. Assuming of course she still lived locally.

He was sure she only saw him as a doctor, but for him, Zara and Finn's birth represented the moment his heart had healed, and he'd forever be indebted to her for that. It was probably only because they'd shared such an intimate moment together after the birth of her son, but he'd felt some weird connection to her that night and no matter how much he'd tried to convince himself he'd imagined it, the closer he got to Glengarrick from the Gold Coast, the stronger the feelings grew.

When Hamish had asked him to find some accommodation for the buck's weekend, Braxton Park had been his first pick because it was so close to Glengarrick. Zara's name wasn't mentioned anywhere on the website and it hadn't been until he'd stopped at the pub to get something to eat and met Zara's mum that she'd told him her daughter owned the property and the pieces had fallen into place.

Closing his eyes, he could still the look on her face when she finally recognised him. Her broad smile had made his blood pound a little faster. The second he'd seen her again, it felt like everything in his world had tilted upside down. It wasn't just a physical attraction, there was an emotional bond that linked them.

The fire needed more kindling, so he grabbed his puffer jacket and headed outside. It was pitch black, but with the number of gum trees near the cottage, it wouldn't be hard to find some smaller pieces of wood to get the fire going. Somewhere in the distance he heard a horse whinny and a second horse neigh in return. He smiled. He'd always loved riding horses. He closed his eyes and inhaled, letting the smell of wet grass infiltrate his senses. He'd lived in the city for the past two years and hadn't realised how much he'd missed the fresh country air.

He'd learned to ride as kid. At first, he hadn't been interested, but his mum insisted that given they lived on a farm, riding a horse was an important skill to have. Once he realised how enjoyable it was, he was the one begging to have his own horse. As a teenager, it had been hard to juggle riding and playing footy and eventually football and his mates had replaced his dreams of riding in the Olympics.

Back inside, he soon had the fire roaring. With nothing else to do, he sank onto the couch and pointed the remote at the television. Nothing. He pushed buttons, wiggled batteries, and checked connections, but after ten minutes, he gave up. Unless he was prepared to call Zara and ask her what he was doing wrong, there wouldn't be any TV. There was no Wi-Fi either and he only had one bar of mobile coverage on his phone. He remembered reading about that in the description of the property online. There was a strong signal further up the hill near the main house where Zara lived, but the cottages were in a dip in the valley and coverage was patchy.

At the time of booking the buck's weekend, two whole days without the internet had sounded like a great idea to all of them, especially Ryan. Unplugging and getting back to nature and away from social media was just what he needed. Hamish and the other guys hadn't been too concerned either. All they wanted to do was drink beer and fish, neither of which required mobile phone reception. But now he was smack dab in the middle of it, reality set in. As much as he didn't want to know what people were saying about him on social media, part of him *did* want to know.

He sighed and tossed his phone on the couch, then scrubbed his beard. If he was being honest, it wasn't necessarily the lack of Wi-Fi that was irritating him; it was the lack of a distraction. He needed to immerse himself in something, anything, to distract himself from Zara.

There was nothing to do except take a shower and fall into bed. He had a feeling he'd be asleep as soon as his head hit the pillow.

Chapter Seven

The sound of laughter and women's voices woke him. It was bright daylight outside, but he had no idea what time it was. He fumbled for his phone to check, but he'd forgotten to plug it in to charge and it was flat. He heard footsteps on the steps leading up to the cottage then someone knocked on the door.

He swung his legs out of bed and called out, 'Coming.'

He hastily pulled on a pair of jeans over his boxer shorts and hurried to the door. He opened it wide. Two surprised faces stared at his bare chest.

Zara's initial look of shock was replaced by laughter and a quick scan of his body, but the teenage girl with her turned bright red and looked away.

'Sorry,' he said, wishing he'd pulled on a t-shirt.

'I wanted to check everything was okay,' Zara said.

He ran his hands through his hair. He'd need to get it cut before the wedding. 'What time is it?'

'Nearly midday.'

He blinked. 'I must have needed the sleep.'

'Are you hungry?'

'Now you mention it, yes.'

'This is Emily,' Zara said, indicating the teenager. 'We were going to see if you wanted to join us for a ride.'

On the submission form for the cottage, he'd ticked the box for the horse-riding experience as part of their weekend getaway. 'Love to, but I'll need a shower first.'

'Well, head up to the house when you're ready and I'll have something for you to eat then we can go for a ride. Do you have boots?'

'Yep.'

'Good. Oh, I had a text from your friend Hamish and they're not expecting to get here until after six so we're not in a hurry.'

'Sounds good.'

Zara stepped back. 'See you soon.'

*

By the time he'd showered and headed to the main house for some food, Emily had gone home. He half expected Zara to cancel her offer of a ride, but as soon as he'd eaten, they'd headed to the stables to saddle up two horses. Not long after, Zara led the way down a gravel road, which they walked along for a few minutes, before turning through an opening in a fence and taking a small trail that wove up into the hills. They didn't talk much as they followed the dirt path up an incline but that didn't bother Ryan. He was just thrilled to be back on a horse and enjoying the view between the horse's ears. And the view of Zara's cute backside. She sat on a horse like she'd been born in the saddle.

It took nearly half an hour of mostly walking and the occasional trot before they broke through the trees into a clearing.

Zara twisted around in the saddle and smiled at him. 'How are you feeling?'

'Great. Loving it.' He nudged the horse in the side until he came up beside Zara and her horse Colby. 'I'm surprised how natural it feels to be back in the saddle.' He chuckled. 'Although I'm sure my legs and backside will be paying for it tomorrow.'

She laughed. 'If you're feeling confident, we can canter later. I just wanted you to get used to Stormy.'

'She's great.' He rubbed the mare's black mane. 'Although I would have thought you'd have chosen an Australian Stock horse instead of a thoroughbred.'

'All my horses are off the track.'

'Off the track? Ex-racehorses?'

She nodded. 'The older ones are great for beginners. They're generally calm and quiet because they've been desensitised at the racetrack.'

'That makes sense, I guess. I always thought they had a reputation for being highly strung.'

Zara chuckled. 'Yeah, they can be crazy, but I've been really fortunate with mine. 'I can't believe you haven't ridden for over ten years,' she said. 'You're doing well.'

'I'd forgotten how much I enjoyed it. Especially on days like this.' He tipped his head back and inhaled the cold mountain air deep into his lungs.

Living on the Gold Coast, he'd missed the crisp winter weather he'd first experienced when he came to Glengarrick. All it had taken was half an hour riding with Zara and he was more relaxed than he had been in the past two months. Sunshine and the scent of dirt and trees never got old.

She moved off and he followed her to a small rise. 'Wow. What an incredible view.'

'It's something else, isn't it?'

Up here, in the wispy fog above the valley, he could almost forget where he was. It was a hazy, hidden realm where just the two of them existed.

'It's unreal.'

Their horses stood like sentinels, as if they, too, were enjoying the view over the valley below. In the distance, mountains stretched into the bright blue sky and to their right, Zara pointed out Glengarrick. The town was mostly buried in early morning fog still, but tendrils of smoke from chimneys wisped into the air.

'I can see why you bought this property. How many acres did you say it is?'

'Twenty-five, but I have direct access to the state forest, which is what we have been riding through, as well as the property next door to mine that backs onto the river.'

'Amazing,' he repeated. And he meant it. 'Do you miss being close to town?'

'Not often. Only when I have a craving for chocolate and Finn is in bed.'

'Where *is* Finn today?'

'With friends of mine. They look after him every Friday so I can have a day off to myself. I usually use the day for grocery shopping and cleaning and all the boring jobs, but I also try to get in a long ride.'

'They sound like good friends.'

She smiled. 'They're the best. Want to head down towards the river?'

He had a feeling she'd just changed the subject, but he also sensed where Finn was concerned, she wasn't willing to give out too much information. Not that it mattered. He was thoroughly enjoying the ease of their conversation. They had so much to talk about, so much in common.

'Do we have time?' he asked, not wanting the ride to end, but also knowing he should be around when the other guys arrived.

'Plenty. It's only two o'clock now.'

'Then I'd love to.' The more time he got to spend alone with Zara before the other guys arrived, the better.

Chapter Eight

When they arrived at the river, Zara dismounted easily from her horse and walked to the water's edge. He followed suit, although he couldn't move as nimbly as she did. She stood with her hands on her hips, staring at the river, which at this point was only a few metres wide. It wove its way through overhanging willows.

'These aren't natives,' he said, pointing to the trees.

'We're back on private property. There used to be a house down here and someone planted them. They're gorgeous, aren't they?'

'Very pretty.'

'If I could afford it, I'd buy this place too.'

He turned his attention upriver and, through a gap in the trees, saw a snow-covered mountain. 'Are we that close to the ski fields?'

She nodded. 'Didn't you go up there when you lived here?'

He shook his head. 'I was only here for the month and it was spring. I was so busy working I didn't really get a chance to check out the district.'

'If only you were staying longer this time. I'd take you up and we could go skiing.'

'Actually—'

She turned around to look at him.

'I didn't tell you yesterday…I was surprised you didn't already know…I've taken Laura Martin's job. It's a twelve-month maternity leave position.'

Zara's eyes lit up. 'That's fantastic.'

Her smile was so large and her response so genuine, the blood in his veins pounded faster. What was wrong with him? Being attracted to a woman wasn't new, but this reaction was. After what he'd been through with Malinda, he thought he was done with women. Maybe not. But with all the baggage he carried, would Zara even be interested in him?

'So tell me about Ryan Dunlop.' Zara asked, surveying him.

'Not much to tell. You already know I'm a doctor.'

'Where were you working before this?'

He hesitated. He'd told this story so many times, but still hated re-telling it.

'I was the club doctor for one of the AFL clubs in Queensland. The Suns.'

Her eyes widened. 'That would have been exciting.'

He shrugged. 'If you're into football.'

'I love the footy.' Her gaze narrowed. 'You don't? I would have thought loving football would have been a prerequisite for a job like that.'

He used to love the game, but since everything that had happened, his passion for it had somewhat soured.

'Ever since I can remember, I had a footy in my hands—bouncing it, tossing it up and marking it, flicking it around, even cradling the ball like a baby when I watched telly. I often wondered if the players who made it to the AFL dreamed of footy the way I did—hoping they'd get to play at the coveted "G".'

'Were you any good?'

'God no.' He chuckled. 'I was an average footballer in high school—played a few games in the firsts—but after Mum died of cancer mid-way through my final year of school, I shifted my focus and decided to become a doctor. Study soon overtook my desire to play kick-to-kick in the backyard with my brother.'

'I'm sorry about your mum. Losing her must have been very tough.'

'It was.' He didn't elaborate. He still missed her so much.

'Where did work once you qualified?'

'A number of different places, including the locum job in Glengarrick where I first met you. Then I was offered my dream job with the Suns. I accepted it without a second's hesitation.'

'Was it a full-time role?'

'No. I managed to juggle a demanding schedule for the club during the footy season with working at a busy bulk billing general practice clinic in Broadbeach at the same time. To say I was busy is an understatement.'

He'd also managed to find time to start—and end, he reminded himself—a relationship. His first serious one since Lisa. But he wasn't going to tell Zara that.

He dragged his mind back to the present. Thinking about the past was too painful and served no purpose.

'So why the change?' she asked.

'I was ready for a break.'

He exhaled slowly. What was the point in holding back the truth? Clearly Zara didn't follow the football. If she did, she'd already know his story. It had been splashed all over the news for a week or so then picked up by social media. 'I got sacked from the club.'

She sat up and stared at him. 'Why?'

'Two of the younger players were selling prescription drugs to other players.'

Her mouth dropped open. 'What? And they blamed you?'

'It's more confusing than that. It turns out my ex-girlfriend, Malinda, who was also a doctor, had a scam going. She used my prescribing rights and ordered drugs for my patients without their knowledge or consent. She was then able to collect them from different pharmacies around Brisbane and the Gold Coast and she sold them to the two players who on-sold them.'

'And you knew nothing about it?'

He shook his head. 'Not a thing. Malinda chose patients of mine with chronic health conditions. If anyone checked, they'd presume the patients actually needed the drugs.'

'I can't believe it. How did she get found out?'

'One of my patients *did* need a drug that required me to get authority to prescribe it. When I made the phone call, I was told the patient had reached her cap for that particular drug. It didn't make sense.'

'But wouldn't Malinda have needed to sign your name?'

'Not with e-scripts. She knew my password on my laptop and just logged into the software.'

'How did you find out it was her?'

'One of the players got caught and pointed the finger at me. The club seized my laptop and of course all the evidence was there. I knew it had to be Malinda, because she was the only one who would have known my password, but she denied it.'

'And you lost your job while she walked? That hardly seems fair.'

It wasn't fair and the pain of it still ate at him. Still, it could be worse. He could have lost his registration. At least he still had that, and now, with the job in Glengarrick, he had a chance to put some space between him and his connections in Queensland. Hopefully, time would heal the wounds.

'Malinda had her issues.'

Zara frowned. 'We all have issues, but that doesn't mean we steal drugs and sell them. Was she using them too?'

'Probably.'

More likely, definitely. Malinda struggled with mental illness—he suspected she was Bipolar, but she refused to seek a diagnosis. If he was truthful with himself, their relationship had started unravelling not long after they got together, and he'd realised he didn't trust her.

At first, he'd wanted to protect Malinda—after what she'd done, she'd probably never practice medicine again—but in order to protect her, he would have had to admit to something he didn't do, and he would have lost his license. In the end, Malinda came clean, but by then the club had sacked him and even though they talked about reinstating him, he was done.

'How long were you and Malinda together?' Zara asked.

'Eighteen months.'

'Was it serious?'

'I thought so. Serious enough we were talking about starting a family.' At least, Malinda had talked about it. He'd been hesitant. Thank goodness he had been.

'Have you been married before?'

He raised his eyebrows. Either Zara had made a good guess, or she was perceptive.

'I figured you're nearly forty. Chances are you've been married before. I can't imagine a guy like you being single.'

'I was married a long time ago.' He didn't elaborate.

'Do you have children?'

'No.' It wasn't technically a lie, but he didn't want Zara's sympathy. It was easier if people didn't know what had happened to him and Lisa.

'Do you want to have children?'

'Absolutely. One day, if the right person comes along again, I'd love to start a family. I'd love to teach my child to ride a horse or kick a footy. It must be awesome watching Finn grow up and see yourself in him.'

Zara shot to her feet and brushed the grass off her backside. 'We should get going.'

He looked up. Her whole demeanour had changed. What had he said wrong?

After mounting their horses, they rode home, mostly in silence, Ryan trying to figure out what he'd said to upset Zara. She replied to his questions, but the ease of their early conversation was gone.

Still, he felt a pang of disappointment when they pulled into the yard near the stables. In a couple of hours, the other guys would arrive, and he was unlikely to get a chance to be alone with Zara again.

After they unsaddled the horses and brushed them down, Zara left to pick up Finn and he wandered back over to the cottage. After a quick shower, he made himself a cup of tea and sat on the back step, enjoying the warmth of the winter sunshine on his face.

He stretched his legs in front of him and stared out at the blue sky above the tree line. The sun slowly dropped, along with the temperature, and he sat in silence broken only by the sound of birdsong.

Calm filtered through as he allowed the evening air to refresh him and ease some of the hell he'd endured in the past few months.

He closed his eyes. Inhaled. Exhaled. This, right here, was better than any therapy. He'd definitely made the right decision to take the job in Glengarrick.

He wasn't sure how long he sat there, but the soft fall of footsteps had him snapping out of his trance-like state. He glanced up to see Zara walking towards him carrying a covered plate, Finn trotting by her side. The smile she offered him didn't seem as forced as it had earlier.

'Did you get the message from Hamish and the other guys?'

He shook his head. 'I don't have much mobile coverage down here, so I've turned my phone off. Must say, it's been blissful not having to keep checking it.'

'He just called. They're going to stop in Glengarrick at the pub for dinner before coming here. He wanted to know if you were here and when I said yes, he asked if I could pass on the message.'

He held back a sigh. 'To be honest the last thing I want to do is go to the pub with them.' He knew he couldn't avoid at least one big night of drinking at the pub—after all it was Hamish's buck's weekend—but he could probably plead off for tonight.

'So, don't go.'

Finn pulled out a couple of old school matchbox cars from his pocket and started driving them through the garden beds. Zara sank onto the step next to Ryan and passed him the plate. He lifted the foil, revealing freshly baked muffins.

'Raspberry and white chocolate. Just out of the oven. It will ruin your dinner, but I figure you've burned off a lot of calories riding this afternoon.'

He took a muffin and held it. 'I know I should go to the pub with them tonight, but it's not really my scene and after such a great day today, it would be nice to just hang here and chill.'

'I get that. I used to love going out but since Finn …' She smiled at the little boy ignoring them both as he played with his cars in the dirt. 'Since Finn, life has changed. And I wouldn't have it any other way,' she added emphatically. 'The only time I go to the pub these days is after a footy match when Glengarrick has won, and the girls drag me there.'

'I think I'm just too old for big booze ups.'

She chuckled. 'How old are you?'

'Forty next year.'

'Spring chicken.'

'Easy to say when you're still in your early thirties.'

He snuck a glance at her. She could have passed for early twenties. She'd taken her hair out of the ponytail she'd worn when riding and it fell over her shoulders. He tried to visualise Zara dressed up for a night out. If she replaced the loose t-shirt with a slim-fitting top and wore makeup, she'd probably get hit on by every red-blooded man in town.

'How do you know Hamish?' she asked, changing the subject. She was an expert at doing that.

'We went to school together, drifted apart through university and bumped into each other a year or so ago. He got a job as one of the physios at the footy club and we started spending time together. We don't really have much in common and I was surprised when he asked me to be in his bridal party.' Although to be fair to Hamish, he was one of the few friends who had stuck around after Ryan walked out on Malinda.

'I'm surprised he'd want to celebrate a buck's party in the middle of country Victoria. Why not in Queensland?'

'His fiancée's parents have a property in the Yarra Valley and that's where the wedding's going to be next weekend.'

'Ah, that makes sense. I was wondering what the connection was.'

'Hamish gave me the job of find something suitable. Braxton Park was the first place that popped up when I searched Facebook for something in Glengarrick.'

She smiled. 'Well, I'm glad I spent extra money doing sponsored ads. They obviously work.'

They sat in silence for a while. Zara finally gave him a nudge. 'Are you going try that muffin or keep using it as a hand warmer?'

At her nod towards the muffin, he took a bite.

'Mmm, good,' he murmured after swallowing a mouthful. 'Did you make these?'

She nodded. 'With some help from Finn.'

Ryan glanced at Finn. 'I presume he washed his hands first.'

Finn's hands clearly hadn't seen soap or water for a while.

'Of course not. Bit of dirt makes them taste better.'

He laughed, relaxing even more around her.

He wasn't a natural flirt when it came to women. Not like Hamish, or some of the other guys he'd known through the footy club. Granted, he'd had more luck with women once he started working at the club—that's where Malinda had first noticed him— but before he dated Malinda, he sometimes felt like talking to women was like taking a test he hadn't studied for. But perhaps that was because with his ex-girlfriend, everything *had* been a test.

Maybe if the timing was right this weekend, he'd tell Zara more of the story. He had a sense she'd listen and not pass judgment. And given he was going to be around for the next year, it would be good to have someone who knew his side of things. Someone who might be willing to stick up for him if the journalists decided to cause problems again. And if he was really brave, he'd tell her about Lisa too.

It was a shame his contract at the clinic was only for a year because he could think of no reason not to ask Zara out on a date. Even if it was just for coffee. Except a voice in the back of his mind warned him Zara probably wasn't the type of girl to be interested in something that already had an end date. Unless Laura decided to extend her maternity leave.

'What are your plans tomorrow?' Zara asked.

'I don't think we have plans. The guys just want to go fishing and drink beer.'

Zara chuckled. 'I was going to say that's not a very cultured way to spend a buck's weekend and was going to suggest you look into going to a local winery or something.'

'Trust me, a winery sounds perfect, but Hamish has it in his head that nothing will beat a weekend of boating, camping and fishing. And riding of course. Are we still able to do that on Sunday?'

'Absolutely. As long as everyone's happy to follow my rules and stay safe.'

'Of course.'

'If you're interested, there's a footy game on tomorrow. Glengarrick Saints are playing. They're on top of the ladder. Haven't lost a game all season.'

'Is that the team Jed Delaney coaches?'

'Uh-huh. You know Jed?'

'Not personally, but by reputation. They say he was one of the best ruckmen to play the game.'

Jed was a big name in the game even though he'd retired a few years earlier after sustaining one too many head injuries.

'Jed's actually married to my friend Georgie. Remember her? You met her the night of Finn's birth.'

'Yeah, I do. I heard he married someone from up this way.'

'And you know of Annabel Norton? She's Annabel Naylor now. She used to play for the "Cats" in the AFLW. If you're interested, you could come and watch the game with us. No pressure, of course.'

He hesitated. He was interested. Even after the incident that had soured his love of the game, it would be fun to watch a local match. Certainly more fun than fishing.

'I probably should check with the guys first.'

Zara stood. 'Like I said, no pressure. Coin toss is at one.' She glanced back towards the house.

'Are you in a hurry to rush off?' he asked, not wanting her to go.

She chewed her lip for a second. 'Not really. Everything's ready for your friends.' She looked at Finn then at her watch. 'But it's getting late, and this little guy needs a bath.'

Ryan followed her gaze. 'He's as happy as the proverbial pig in mud. Look at him. He's having fun.' He gestured to the spot on the step next to him. 'Can you stay for a few more minutes? I really enjoyed spending time with you today, Zara, and it would be nice to have some company to watch the sun set.'

Her cheeks pinked. 'I…I suppose I can.'

Did he imagine the waver in her voice?

She sat beside him, so close their thighs touched for a split second before she shifted away.

'Tomorrow night you and the other guys should go up the mountain and watch the sun set from there. It's spectacular.'

'If you ask me, the view is pretty darn good right here.'

She poked his arm and rolled her eyes, and he was more than happy to take it.

Chapter Nine

Sitting so close to Ryan, Zara's heart felt like it was skipping every second beat.

'No pressure,' he said.

She hesitated briefly then asked herself what was wrong with the simple joy of sharing a moment in time with a decent, kind man. Sure, watching a sun set was the type of romantic thing the hero and heroine in books did, not something she'd ever done, but if nothing else, it was nice to have the adult company.

They sat in silence and when she shivered—not from the cold, but from the nearness of him—he jumped up and grabbed one of the blankets off the couch inside, returning and wrapping it around her shoulders. It was such a thoughtful gesture, something no-one had ever done for her, that she felt herself softening towards him even further. The only other guy she knew who treated women like this was Ben.

As the sun sank lower and lower, she tried to tell herself not to get attached to Ryan. He was only staying around for a year. And, the kicker, he'd told her how much he wanted a family of his own—something she could never give him.

'If I lived out here I'd want to sit and watch every sunset,' Ryan said finally, breaking the silence.

'It's good to see them through someone else's eyes. I forgot how wonderful they are.'

She tried to steady her breathing but every time she inhaled, she lemony scent of Ryan's bodywash tickled her senses. If he'd asked her what the sunset was like, she wouldn't have been able to describe it. It was taking all her concentration to try to banish the disorientation that seemed to have taken over her body.

'Absolutely beautiful.'

Something in his voice made her twist around to stare at him. He wasn't looking at the sky, but directly at her.

Her face flame and she opened her mouth to say something, but nothing came out. Swallowing, she stood and brushed off the back of her jeans. 'It's late. I should get to bed.'

Ryan stood too and opened his arms for a hug.

She hugged him in return knowing there was no chance her sleep tonight wouldn't be full of thoughts of him and the way she felt when his arms were around her.

*

The next morning, after a surprisingly sound sleep, Zara woke and headed out to feed the horses. Smoke curled out of the chimney of Ryan's cottage and she saw a light on but no movement. The other cottage was still dark.

After giving Finn his breakfast, she fed the horses then got Finn rugged up and ready to go into town. As she secured him in his car seat, she caught the taillights of a car heading down the driveway. No doubt the men had decided to head into Glengarrick to get a late breakfast. She followed them, trying to stop thinking about Ryan, but it was impossible. He filled every thought.

The main street of Glengarrick was the beating heart of the town. Over the years the old shop fronts had been restored and nowadays tourists happily blended with locals as they meandered along the street, take away coffee cups in hand as they explored the quirky gift and clothing stores. Most locals understood that 'city folk' were crucial to the economy of Glengarrick and were friendly and welcoming.

After dropping Finn off at her mum's house, she headed for The Silver Spoon. Georgie's café. It was by far the best place in town for good coffee, which meant it was likely Ryan and the guys would be eating breakfast there this morning. She braced herself emotionally, just in case.

A bell jangled as she opened the old wooden door and entered the café. It was early, but the place was abuzz with chatter and laughter. She inhaled deeply, taking in the scent of freshly baked bread and ground coffee beans. The decor included artwork by local artists and on the back wall was a blackboard displaying the menu, which Zara knew by heart. In one corner, a large wood-burning stove was pumping out heat in the large space. Comfy couches and a coffee table were set in front of the fire and that's where Ryan and his friends sat. None of them looked up when she walked in.

Georgie was behind the counter and she waved and smiled as soon as she saw Zara.

'Good morning. Where's my little man?'

'I just dropped him off to Mum and Dad. He's going to have a sleepover with them tonight. You know Finn. He's beside himself with excitement.'

Georgie chuckled. 'I know your folks. They'll be as thrilled as Finn.'

'Absolutely.'

'Are you here for breakfast?'

'No, thanks. Just a takeaway coffee please. I ate at home earlier and I'll grab a sausage at the game.'

While Georgie made her coffee, Zara stared at the glass display cabinet filled with tempting delights. She had no intention of buying any of the decadent chocolate brownies or even the healthier sugar-free bliss balls and slices. Staring at the food stopped her from staring at Ryan and his friends.

As soon as she had her coffee, she headed back outside and walked purposefully towards the football ground. She loved the football and went to every home game. As much as she was able, she also tried to get to the away games too. Sometimes her parents would bring Finn down for the last quarter, but he was too young to appreciate the game, and ended up being a distraction to everyone.

Hopefully today, watching the game would keep her mind where it needed to be.

Chapter Ten

The umpire bounced the ball, and the opposing rucks went at it. Zara leaned on the fence at the boundary line, anticipating the Glengarrick Saints to be the first to kick it out of the centre. The team was really strong this year and hadn't lost a game yet.

Archer Lawson, Glengarrick's ruckman, kicked it out to the wing and three players raced after it. It was two against one and although a Saint's player got to it first, the kick sent it over the line and out of bounds.

The umpire threw the ball back in and Glengarrick's AFL hopeful, Dave Morrison, snared it and got in a quick kick. Bodies collided and the ball disappeared from view in a flurry of hands and feet. One of the Saints scooped it out.

'That's a throw,' a spectator shouted, his voice ringing out over the ground. Zara glanced over and saw Pete Williams.

The umpire clearly didn't agree and play continued.

The next few minutes of the game were played at a fast and furious pace.

'They look nervous,' Wendy Matthews said.

'They'll be fine, love. Just finding their feet. Ground's so dry,' her husband replied.

'We could use some rain,' Roger, the old bloke who had the farm closest to Zara said.

She nodded too. Every time a player landed in the dirt, the thump of the man's body against the solid surface made her wince.

The ball was kicked out on the full and there was a delay while one of the kids chased after it and kicked it back to the umpire. The majority of the action for the next few minutes was on the other side of the ground from where Zara stood. She took her eyes off the play to glance around the ground, hoping to catch a glimpse of Ryan and his mates. When she couldn't spot them in the crowd, she felt a wave of disappointment wash her over even though she had told Ryan there was no pressure to come.

And fair enough, local footy probably wasn't that interesting to someone used to watching the AFL. It would be pretty boring for Ryan and his friends who had already said they were here to sit around and fish and drink beer.

She turned her attention back to the game. The ball was thrown in again and knocked over the back of another player.

'There's no-one there!' Roger shouted.

'They've just missed another opportunity,' Wendy replied as Archer gave his opponent a shove in the chest before pushing off and accelerating towards the ball.

The ruck from the other team got to the ball before him and gave it a quick kick out to the centre—straight into the arms of a Glengarrick player.

A cheer went up from the crowd.

'That's a beautiful piece of work,' Bob Tomkins stated. Zara held back a chuckle. Bob was legally blind and nearly ninety.

Archer crossed the fifty-metre line, bounced the ball then looked for a teammate to kick it to. One of the men came forward, Archer kicked it straight to him and he marked it cleanly before promptly turning around and popping it through the goals.

The first score of the game was to the Saints and it had everyone on their feet, punching the air. Car horns blared and players ran from everywhere, slapping the goal-kicker on the back and high fiving each other.

Someone in the Saints cheer squad started up a chant and the supporters joined in. The crowd was three to one in favour of local Saints team.

'Check out Lawson's mum,' Wendy said.

Zara smiled as she looked over at Jenny Lawson at her usual spot behind the goals, jumping up and down, shaking huge blue and white pom poms. She was one of Glengarrick's most fervent followers.

'First goal doesn't mean a victory,' a man said.

Zara glanced over at him. She didn't recognise him and figured he was from the opposition.

'You know what they say. First out, last home,' he said.

'We'll see if that holds true today.' Zara smiled at him before turning her attention back to the game.

Two Glengarrick players moved up towards the wing and it became obvious the first goal had given them all a boost.

Lawson tapped the ball out after the next centre bounce and Digby Smith, who was the youngest player on the ground, controlled it with the skill of someone twice his age and got a quick handball out. The opposition player slipped over, allowing Glengarrick to get the ball out wide and then on quickly to where Jimmy, their half-forward flank was waiting. He swooped, dodging two players and banged the ball through for the Saint's second goal.

The opposing team didn't like it and a bit of jumper punching ensued.

'They'll 'ave to be careful,' Roger said. 'Umpies won't let that go on for too long.'

A couple of small skirmishes broke out over the ground, but the umpires quickly regained control and the game continued.

With a few minutes of play left, Glengarrick were up by ten points and that's when Zara spotted Ryan. He was with his mates, on the other side of the ground. As if sensing her eyes on him, he looked up and caught her gaze. A smile broke out across his face and he waved. She waved back. Someone jostled her and when she looked back Ryan was gone.

Moments later the siren sounded, and cheers erupted. Glengarrick had won another game. Rather than head back to her car, Zara walked around the ground to where the team had gathered around Jed, their coach.

Steam rose from the men's bodies, filling the air and mixing with the smell of mud, menthol and sweat. The teams lined up and shook hands with the opposition before bursting into the club's theme song. The mood among the locals around the ground was euphoric and Zara was swept up in it.

'Great job, boys, that's it. Good job. Well done.' Jed clapped players on the back as they passed him.

The other team made their way towards the change rooms, mostly in silence, their boots click-clacking on the concrete. They were strong and fit, but once again Glengarrick was the better team on the day. At this rate, it seemed another premiership cup was a shoe in.

Jed caught sight of her and waved.

'Great game,' she called out to him.

'Thanks, Zars. Good to see you. You going to the pub tonight with the girls?'

'I'll see.'

As she turned to walk back to her car, the last of the Saints players, a group of five who looked barely old enough to shave, trotted past her.

A voice came from the middle of the pack. 'Nice rack, sweetheart.'

Anger ripped through her. She turned, ready to give the guys an earful, when a voice made her freeze.

'Oi! Stop!'

Ryan.

The boys pulled up and turned to stare at him. Zara expected to see one or two offer sheepish looks, but instead, arrogance came off them in waves.

Her blood boiled and she was about to demand who'd made the comment when Ryan stepped up to the group.

'Who said that?' Ryan glared at the offenders.

Silence.

'Who made that comment?' he repeated.

'It was just a joke, man. Nothin' in it,' one of the players said.

Judging by the looks on their faces, no one was about to own up. Zara was about to tell Ryan not to worry about it, but his face was stony and his blue eyes flashed dark.

'Right then. Fifty burpees. All five of you,' he said, voice like flint.

'Says who?'

'Yeah, who the hell are you?'

Jed appeared, frowning. 'What's going on?'

'This jerk wants us to do burpees.'

Ryan folded his arms over his chest and glared at them. 'The only jerk here is you, buddy. If you can't treat women with respect, you can face the consequences.'

Jed looked from Ryan to Zara then walked to Zara's side. 'What's going on?' he muttered.

She shrugged. 'It's no big deal.'

'Who's the guy?'

'Ryan Dunlop.'

Jed frowned. 'The new doctor?'

Zara nodded.

Jed strode over to Ryan, hand outstretched. They shook hands and Ryan stepped away with Jed and lowered his voice. Zara fumed. Obviously Ryan was explaining what had happened but she couldn't hear his words. It didn't matter. Whatever he was saying was evidently enough to upset Jed too.

Jed turned and glared at the five young men in front of him. 'Burpees sounds like the least you can do.'

No-one moved.

'If you want to act like a bunch of high school kids, getting off on a woman's figure, and feeling like you have the right to remark on it, you can get going and keep going, the lot of you. If that's how you want to behave, don't bother turning up for next week's game. Or the one after that.'

He was met with five stunned looks.

'You think I'm joking?' Jed asked. 'This woman is one of my best friends.'

Heavier silence.

By now some of the other players had turned around to see what was happening. Ryan glared at all of them. Zara wasn't sure whether she wanted to sink into the ground in embarrassment, or hug Ryan for standing up for her.

'Yeah, that's right—if any of you ever think you have the right to comment on a woman's breasts—or any part of her anatomy—you can go,' Jed barked. Zara had never seen him lose his temper or raise his voice. 'I only want real men on this team.'

The ruckman, Archer, who was also the captain, stared at his five teammates. 'You heard coach. Burpees. Now.'

Five exhausted bodies dropped to the ground and Archer started counting. Before they'd got to fifteen, Ryan stalked off.

Zara didn't know whether to follow him or stay, but judging by the look on Jed's face, he wasn't finished with ripping through his players, and she didn't feel like hanging around to hear that.

She jogged to catch up to Ryan, calling out his name.

He slowed his stride but kept walking.

'Ryan. Stop.'

He finally stopped and turned.

'I'm sorry. I didn't mean to make a scene.'

She put a hand on his arm. 'Thank you.'

He looked at her.

'Thank you for standing up for me. I don't think anyone's ever done that.'

'I'm sorry,' he repeated. 'It just infuriated me that they could comment on your body like that.'

It wasn't in Zara to make light of the player's comment. After having her breasts removed and reconstructed, she had too much emotional baggage to just laugh it off.

'Boys like them need to learn that comments like that are unacceptable. Half the problems we had at the Suns involved kids who needed to learn how to be men. And that starts with treating women with respect.'

Someone called Zara's name from the other side of the car park and she stifled a groan when she saw Iris Wallace. The seventy-something-year-old was Glengarrick football club's secretary and the town's most active busybody. She was deaf as a post which meant she shouted all the time with a voice worse than fingernails down a blackboard.

Iris hurried over as quickly as her legs could carry her. 'Dr Dunlop, I'm glad I caught you.' She greeted Zara then looked back to Ryan.

'How can I help you?' Ryan asked.

'Oh, you can't help me, but I can help you. I have a proposition for you that I think you'll love. I heard you're coming back to take Laura's position at the clinic and I'm presuming you don't have anywhere to live. Jodie and I have a spare room at our place.'

'Is Jodie back in town?' Zara asked.

Iris nodded.

'For good?'

Jodie was single and Iris was a matchmaker. This "proposition" had disaster written all over it. But how could she warn Ryan without appearing rude?

'Why don't you come for dinner one night next week?' Iris asked, cocking her head to one side. 'My Jodie makes a mean pavlova, and I can put on a lamb roast if you'd like.'

'Thanks for the offer, Iris. That's very kind of you. I had been wondering what I was going to do about accommodation.'

'Which is why I offered Ryan one of the cottages at my place,' Zara said, smiling sweetly at Iris.

Ryan's head flicked around to look at her. She gave him a look she hoped he'd interpret as "don't say another word".

Iris frowned. 'But your cottages are short term holiday rentals. They're not suited for a doctor to live in. And you're too far out of town.'

'Ryan needs somewhere to keep his horse too.'

Beside her, she could almost hear Ryan's unspoken questions, but he wisely kept quiet. Iris didn't need to know he didn't have a horse. Or a clue what was going on.

'I still think our place would be much more suitable. And Jodie would be happy to cook meals for Dr Dunlop.'

'I think you'll find Ryan is more than capable of cooking for himself.'

'I do enjoy cooking,' Ryan agreed.

Iris harrumphed.

Ryan gave her a big smile. 'But I totally appreciate your offer, and perhaps once I'm settled, Zara and I could come over and enjoy that roast lamb.'

Zara quickly turned her snort of laughter into a cough. Jodie couldn't stand her, so there'd be no invite for dinner forthcoming.

'Well, I suppose so. And of course, if it doesn't work living *so far* out of town, you can always change your mind.'

'Of course.' Ryan smiled at her again.

'We'd better keep going,' Zara said. She glanced up at the sky. Dark clouds had formed. 'Looks like it's going to rain.'

'Goodnight, then,' Iris said before turning and walking away.

When Iris was out of earshot, Ryan asked, 'Since when do I have a horse?'

Zara giggled. 'Trust me, you'll have a stable full of horses before I let Jodie Wallace get her claws into you. That girl is a nightmare. I don't know how many relationships she's had, but none of them last longer than a few months. She tends to come back to Glengarrick when she gets dumped, then she's off again when she finds someone else. Internet dating, from what I hear. All I can say is there's no love lost between us.'

'Oh. Right.'

'And I guarantee as soon as Iris knew you were coming back to Glengarrick, she asked Jodie to hot-foot it home.'

'I could put them all at rest and let them know I'm not interested in a relationship.'

Zara filed that bit of information away. 'Might be a good idea.' With his good looks and charming personality, single women would no doubt be lining up for a "check-up" with the doctor.

They were almost at Ryan's car when Jed jogged over to them. 'Sorry about the boys, Zara,' he said, when he got closer. 'I had a word to them. Won't happen again.'

'Thanks, Jed. To be honest, it really angered me.'

'Yeah, well it angered us too.' Jed turned to Ryan and held out his hand. 'Wish we'd met under better circumstances. I hear you're going to be the new doc in town.'

Ryan nodded. 'Yeah, just for the year. Laura's taken maternity leave.'

'You're always welcome down at the club. Would be good to have someone who knows what they're talking about. Some of these kids get knocked out or injured and won't believe me when I say they have to take a couple of weeks off. They might listen to you.'

'You obviously don't know my story.'

'I know what was reported on the news. The club let you go after they found out some of the younger players were dealing prescription drugs.'

'He wasn't charged with anything,' Zara said.

'Not that you'd know that if you read the comments on social media,' Ryan said.

'I don't get involved in all that rubbish.'

'Good to know. For a while it was trial by Twitter.'

'It was your wife wasn't it?' Jed asked.

Ryan shook his head. 'Girlfriend. Malinda. She eventually admitted it, but by then I'd already been sacked by the club. There was some talk behind the scenes about getting my job back, but I was done.'

'Sounds like you moved here to get away from it all,' Jed said.

'Something like that. Fresh start. I remembered how much I enjoyed it when I was here filling in at the clinic two years ago. It seemed fortuitous that a position opened up when I needed it.'

'It's fate,' Zara agreed.

'If you're happy to come down and meet the boys, I'd love to have you on board,' Jed said.

'Yeah, well, after today I don't know whether I'd have their respect.'

'On the contrary, what you did today was exactly what they needed. I'd be stoked if you wanted to come down and help out.'

'Let me have a think about it. It'll depend how busy I am at the clinic.'

Jed beamed. 'Sounds good. Anyway, changing the subject. What are your plans tonight? I know the girls are going to the pub, so Ben and I were planning to have a few quiet beers and watch the Bombers game on telly if you want to join us.'

'Thanks for the invite but I'm actually here with some friends this weekend. It's my mate's buck's weekend and I think they were planning to go to a pub tonight anyway, so I'll probably go with them.'

'Only one pub in town, so I'll see you there anyway.' Jed shook Ryan's hand and jogged off.

'He seems like a nice guy.'

'He's the best,' Zara said. 'You'll love getting to know all my friends.'

'Were you serious about the cottage?' he asked.

'I don't see why not.' She'd made the offer with no consideration of what it would mean to her finances. A drop of rain fell, and she shivered. She needed to get home and have a hot shower. 'We'll talk about it after this weekend. I'm sure we can work something out.'

Chapter Eleven

It was just after seven when Ryan pulled up at The Old Bush Inn, and the heavens opened. There were only a couple of parking spots left in the pub's carpark, and when Hamish and the other two groomsmen got out of the car, the four of them dashed through the downpour. A handful of people stood outside under the veranda getting some fresh air despite the cold temperature. Their gazes drifted towards Ryan and the other guys before deciding they weren't that interesting.

Ryan had offered to be the designated driver so the others could drink, and they'd happily started earlier that afternoon. He'd promised he'd have one or two drinks, but that was it. Pubs and clubs just weren't his scene.

Once inside, they made their way to the bar where they were directed to an available table in a small cosy room just off the main part of the bar.

It was busy, which shouldn't have surprised him considering the local footy team had won today. With the outdoor heaters on, the partially enclosed space was quite warm despite the cold temperature.

In one corner, a guy sat at a keyboard, accompanying a brunette with a great voice singing a cover of a song he recognised but couldn't name. The volume was at a level that ensured patrons could still carry on their conversations.

A waiter was at their side almost at once. 'What can I get you gentlemen?' she asked pleasantly.

Hamish flashed a flirting smile. 'Depends what you're offering.'

Her smile didn't falter.

Ryan leaned in and got her attention. 'We'll start with whatever you have on tap for these guys. I'll have a lemon, lime and bitters.'

'What about a pale ale?' she asked.

'Sounds good. Can we set up a tab?'

'Of course.'

The waitress was back within minutes with their drinks. Hamish downed most of his beer straight away then leaned back in his chair and surveyed the room. 'Not much talent.'

'Mate,' Rob said, 'eyes off. You're getting married next weekend, remember?'

'Doesn't mean I can't have a good weekend.'

'Yeah, well we promised Kim we'd watch out for you,' Dan replied.

Ryan exhaled silently. At least he wasn't going to be the only one keeping Hamish on the straight and narrow.

'Nothing stopping us from chatting to the locals,' Hamish said.

Rob and Dan pushed back their chairs. 'Nothing stopping us at all. You coming Ryan?' Dan asked over his shoulder.

'I'll sit this one out.'

And the next one. And the one after that. He was more than content to sit alone, nursing a lemon, lime and bitters, and watching the crowd. Gazing over at Hamish, Rob and Dan and a group of young men surrounded by a swarm of scantily clad girls who looked barely old enough to be in the pub, Ryan felt every one of his nearly forty years.

Over at the bar the beer was flowing as fast and heavy as the rain bucketed down outside. The large screen television set over the bar was showing the Bombers versus Dockers game and a lot of people in the pub had their heads—or at least their ears—turned towards it. With every goal kicked by the West Australian team, the cluster of noisy drinkers jeered. Like most people in small Victorian country towns like Glengarrick, locals liked to see a Victorian team win even if it wasn't their own.

Ryan was miles away when someone placed another beer on the table in front of him. He glanced up at the tall, skinny man standing there.

He clapped Ryan on the back and his smile revealed a missing front tooth.

'G'day, mate. You'd be the new doc they tell me.'

'That's right, I am.'

'I'm Tony Stevens. Call me Tubby.' He patted a flat stomach. 'Nickname stuck when I was in primary school.'

Ryan offered a smile. 'Nice to meet you.'

Tubby pulled a spare chair closer with his foot and sat, uninvited. He took a swig of his beer and started chatting about the day's game.

Ryan tried to laugh along with Tubby who was an excellent storyteller with comedic timing, but the volume of the music had increased now causing more shouted conversations. The laughter around him was causing a dull buzz in his head, and he found himself staring blankly at the scuffed timber floor instead of at Tubby.

'Hope you don't mind. I ordered something to eat,' Tubby said.

'Sure. Whatever. That's fine.'

Not for the first time, he wished Hamish and the others had gone along with his suggestion to have a quiet night around the outdoor firepit back at the cottages.

'You on your own then?'

'No.' Ryan pointed to where Hamish and Dan were chatting to a group of girls. He couldn't see Rob. 'I'm here with those guys. Buck's party.'

When Tubby's steak arrived, he tucked into it, keeping up a running commentary about everything related to the Glengarrick Football Club between mouthfuls. Thankfully Ryan didn't have to say much. Tubby seemed happy with the occasional nod.

The game on the television ended as Tubby finished eating. The Dockers had won. Tubby stood, held out his hand to shake Ryan's and wandered off.

Not long afterwards, the pub slowly emptied. Probably the regulars heading home. Ryan glanced over to his friends. The boys were still going strong, getting rowdier with each round of beers. Dan had a girl in his lap but thankfully Hamish seemed to be keeping his hands to himself.

He cast his gaze around the pub and noticed four women enter, one of whom was Zara. They headed to the back of the pub and secured a table. The other three women were clearly locals too, as the waitstaff greeted them all with hugs.

Zara looked soft and feminine in a skirt and boots. Her blonde hair was curled in ringlets around her shoulders and she'd clearly done her makeup. Her eyes were dark and her lips red. She looked incredible, but it wasn't just her smile that lit that corner of the room; it was also the way she spoke to the other girls around the table. She was clearly telling a story and the others were hanging off every word. At one point she threw back her head and laughed.

He'd thought her pretty before, but the way she was laughing with her friends took her to more than beautiful. A knockout. And she had no idea that other men in the pub were watching her and noticing her just like he was.

Ryan only realised he was staring at her like a fool when her gaze swung to his side of the room and landed on him.

Their eyes connected and though her laughter died on her lips, her smile didn't dim. Pleasure registered in her eyes, and she hesitated a moment before saying something to her friends and making her way through the crowd to him.

'Hey. Some buck's weekend if they've gone and left you here on your own.'

She pulled out the empty chair Tubby had vacated and sat. Just her proximity doubled the rate of his heartbeat.

He pointed to the other side of the room where the guys had joined a group of other men and women on the dance floor. The pianist and singer were finished, and a DJ was playing dance tunes.

Zara tilted her head and screwed up her nose. 'Not sure the Old Bush Inn has seen so many men in skinny-leg chinos before. But I'm glad they're having a good time.'

He chuckled. 'I don't think they'll be up for a ride tomorrow morning though. I reckon there will be some sore heads.' He cleared his throat and nodded towards her group of friends. 'You having a girl's night out or celebrating something in particular?'

'Just our regular catch up when the Saints win. Georgie and I have been best friends forever, and the other girl is Annabel— she's the one who played AFLW. The fourth girl is Emma. Sometimes Kate joins us too. To be honest, I nearly didn't come tonight, but I'm glad I did.' She glanced over at the dance floor. 'Why don't you join your friends on the dance floor?' she asked.

'Yeah, nah. No thanks. I'm not good at dancing.'

'Is that right?' She grinned. 'Maybe you just haven't had the right partner.'

Her eyes twinkled with amusement and a hint of challenge. Her cheeks were flushed, and her red lips curved into a smile. Was she flirting with him? God, he really wished he were better at picking up on these things. He hesitated, trying to figure out how to respond to her comment. Was he supposed to ask her to dance?

'I should get back to the girls, before they start to gossip about us.' She stood and smoothed her top down. 'Enjoy the rest of the night.'

'Yeah, you too,' he replied, but she'd already walked back to her table.

'Can I get you another drink?' the waitress asked, holding a serving tray tucked against her side.

'That'd be great. Thanks. I might have a beer this time.'

To avoid staring at Zara for the rest of the night, he turned his attention to the dance floor and tried to concentrate on enjoying the music. He should have asked her to dance.

Chapter Twelve

Zara had noticed Ryan the moment she'd walked into the pub. It was hard not to notice him. There was something sexy about a quiet, unassuming man who didn't seem in any hurry to join the hype and partying atmosphere surrounding him. Ryan stood out, but not in a bad way.

When she returned to the table, the girls had already settled in for a big night. 'Who's up for another round of drinks?' Annabel asked. 'This one's on me.'

'Not for me,' Zara said, putting her hand over her glass. 'I'm driving.' She usually offered to be the designated driver because early mornings with Finn and hangovers didn't mix. One glass of champagne was enough.

'It's a yes for me,' Georgie said. 'I can walk home from here.'

'I'm in too,' Emma said. 'As long as Zara doesn't mind dropping me home.'

'Not at all,' Zara replied.

Annabel headed to the bar to order their drinks and the other girls started chatting about a new show on Foxtel they were hooked on. Zara tried hard to concentrate and keep linked into the conversation, but she couldn't stop sneaking glances across the room at Ryan.

'Is he one of the guests staying in the cottages, or someone you know?'

'Hmm?' Zara dragged her attention back to Annabel who had returned to the table. 'Who?'

'That guy sitting over there on his own.' Annabel nodded towards Ryan. 'The one you were chatting with before. You can't stop looking at him.'

'I can't work out where I've seen him before. He looks familiar,' Georgie said.

'He's one of the guests. He's here with his friends for a buck's weekend. But actually, he's also the new locum doctor, taking over from Laura.' Hopefully she sounded as nonchalant as she intended, because her pulse was doing irrational little loop-de-loops.

Georgie's eyes widened. 'Now I remember. It's Dr Delicious.'

Zara gave a tiny nod then with her eyes begged Georgie not to say another word. Hopefully the others hadn't heard Georgie's comment, or she'd have a lot of explaining to do.

'I bet he'll get a lot of new female patients,' Emma said with a giggle. 'He's incredibly good looking although he could lose the beard and get a haircut.'

'He is delicious,' Georgie agreed, with a wink in Zara's direction, 'although don't tell Jed I said so.'

Emma was watching Zara carefully, and she had a suspiciously pensive look on her face. 'Do *you* think he's good looking, Zara?'

'I guess so. I hadn't really noticed.' But the blush that went straight to her cheeks betrayed her words. 'I mean he's hot if you like that scruffy look.'

'Or if you like men,' Emma added, giving Zara another funny look. 'I didn't think you were into men.'

'I like men.'

'And women?' Emma asked.

Zara shrugged. None of her friends had given her a hard time about her sexual preferences in the past so she wasn't sure why Emma was being funny about it now. As far as Zara knew, all her friends accepted her for who she was.

'To be honest, I haven't looked at a woman that way in a long time,' she said.

'You haven't looked at *anyone* that way in a long time,' Georgie said.

'I've been kind of busy,' Zara said, doing her best to be wry rather than resentful. 'I had a baby, battled cancer, had my boobs removed, then had them put back on.'

Georgie put her hand on her arm. 'I know, honey. And you've done an amazing job. So good in fact, it's time you stretched yourself just a little further.' She smiled. 'And I'm sorry if what I said came out wrong. I wasn't having a go at you.'

'Would you be interested?' Emma asked. 'Like, interested enough to ask him out?'

Their drinks arrived and Zara wished she'd ordered another one. The girls kept looking at her then over at Ryan and she knew they weren't going to let this drop easily.

'I don't know if I'd be interested to be honest,' Zara replied. Until Ryan had walked back into her life she'd given zero consideration to having a relationship with anyone other than Finn. Her life was full enough with him in it and she couldn't imagine bringing a third person into the mix.

Emma leaned forward. 'What were you chatting to him about when you went over before?'

Zara lifted a shoulder. 'Just checking he didn't need a ride home.' The lie slipped easily from her lips.

'Well, I think he's hot,' Emma said. 'And if you're not interested, I might have to go and introduce myself.'

Zara gave a small laugh, but something about the way Emma was unashamedly checking out Ryan bothered her.

'Why don't you ask him to dance, Zara?' Georgie's soft words drifted across the table.

Zara swung her gaze back to her best friend. 'Should I?'

'I don't see why not. What would it hurt?'

Maybe nothing. Maybe everything. But she wasn't going to sit back and watch Emma make a move on him.

She stood, pushed her hair over her shoulders and made her way across the room, but not before she saw Emma's mouth drop open and Georgie's look of approval.

Before she reached the table, Ryan turned to look her way. He must have seen the purpose in her eyes, because he set his drink down and sat up straighter.

'Are you here to bug me about dancing again?'

Her face flamed and for a second she was sure he was going to refuse her. Her stomach dropped to her feet and her skin itched with embarrassment. Just when she was wishing she could sink through the floor, he pushed back his chair and stood.

'Righto then, let's dance.'

Zara pictured the look of surprise on Emma's face when Ryan placed his hand on her back and walked them to the crowded dance floor. Tingles raced through her where his fingers touched her.

It didn't take more than a few seconds of moving to the music for her nerves to dissolve into amusement. Ryan wasn't a terrible dancer, but he wasn't good either.

'I told you I couldn't dance,' he said over the music.

'I've seen worse.' She grinned and grabbed his hands, helping him move to the two-step beat. 'Just listen and move to the beat.'

He followed her lead and by the end of the second song, he was smiling and relaxing a bit more as they danced. Just when he was getting the hang of it, the song ended and the next one came on. It was a slow one. Slow dancing was a totally different game, and she wasn't sure she wanted to play. She took a step back, ready to make her escape. Or at least give Ryan the option of calling it quits and going back to his table.

'You're not going to abandon me now, are you?' There was a glint in his eyes. 'Not when I'm just getting the hang of things.'

She glanced back over at her friends. 'Perhaps I should get back to my girlfriends.'

'Stay. Please.'

She smiled. 'When you ask so nicely, how can I refuse?'

He slid an arm around her waist and caught her hand with his free one. When he pulled her flush against him the air in her lungs locked. Light-headed, she was all too aware of her soft curves pressed against the hard lines of his body. The way their hips bumped against each other. The way her knees were threatening to buckle right now. It had to be the one glass of champagne she'd had. It must have gone straight to her head. Yes, it was totally the champagne. She wouldn't accept any other reason.

'I'm glad you asked me to dance,' he said. 'Much better than trying to look like I was having a good time. If you hadn't come over when you did I was about to start scrolling through Facebook.'

The idea of Ryan on Facebook had her laughing, which was a good distraction from the sensation of his long fingers laced through hers. 'At least your phone has reception here in town. It must be tempting to get your phone out and check messages and stuff.'

'No.' His eyes dropped to her mouth. 'That's not what's tempting me right now.'

Hot and cold rushed through her and her throat went dry. *Time to go*. Alarm bells rang in her head. But try as she might, she couldn't stop staring at his lips. Without meaning to, she leaned closer, tilting her head back.

That was the only invitation Ryan needed. His head dipped, blocking out the lights above them as his mouth gently settled on hers. Even though the kiss was tender, her heart slammed into her chest, like a caged bird. She moaned softly and he brushed his lips against hers several times, not rushing the kiss, but making her desperate for a deeper taste of him. She'd imagined his beard would be coarse and uncomfortable, but it was softer than she expected. Just rough enough to graze against her sensitive flesh and make goose bumps rise on her skin.

When she shivered and swayed against him, his lips pressed against hers more firmly and she opened her mouth, helpless against his exploration. Her head spun as she kissed him back, teasing his tongue with hers. Heat spread through her body, gathering low in her belly, and forming an ache of need she hadn't felt in years.

'Nice one, Dunny.'

They sprang apart as Hamish slapped Ryan on the back.

'I think I need some air,' she whispered unsteadily.

Breaking out of Ryan's grip, she threaded her way through the crowd to the exit. What if her parents had seen her kissing Ryan? She had to live in this town, and he had to work here. Neither of them could afford this complication. When she finally made it through the door, there were a handful of people smoking and she moved away from them, making her way to the car park at the back of the building.

The car park was well lit, and she headed to the back corner where she could hide under a canopy of gum trees. Only then, when she was out of sight, was she able to steal a breath. It had stopped raining, but it was cold, and she wished she had her coat. She couldn't hide out here for long or the others would come looking for her then she'd have more explaining to do.

Gravel crunched as footsteps approached. Zara lifted her head, knowing who it was even before she saw him.

'I'm sorry, Zara,' he began hesitantly. 'I must have misread—'

'Don't apologise,' she said, interrupting him.

He frowned. 'But I can tell you're upset and I'm sorry if I'm the cause of that.'

'It's my fault.' She gave a self-conscious laugh. 'There's not a person in that pub tonight who's seen me make out with a guy on the dance floor.'

'Yeah, well, it's not something I usually do either.'

'Make out with guys?'

'You know what I mean. I don't make out with women in public. Ever.'

She tilted her head. 'Ever?'

'I'm not generally good with public displays of affection.' A small smile played across his lips. 'Although I'm glad I made an exception tonight.'

Embarrassment lanced through her again. How many people had seen them kissing? News like this would go through town quicker than a bushfire on a windy, forty-degree day. And if it got back to her parents, they'd be thrilled. Her parents had been outwardly supportive of her previous relationship, but deep down they'd wanted her to commit to a man not a woman.

'And, if I'm honest Zara, the only thing stopping me from kissing you again is I can tell I've upset you.'

She nibbled her bottom lip. 'I'm just not sure it's appropriate.'

'Because I'm a guest?'

'That. And because you're about to be the town's new doctor. The last thing you need is everyone asking you questions about me.'

'It sounds like an excuse to me. And I've dealt with the public spotlight for the last two months. I can cope if someone wants to ask me why I was seen kissing you at the pub.'

She flushed again. 'Ryan, there are a lot of other women who are a lot better for you than me. Trust me. I could introduce you to half a dozen of them if you wanted me to.'

'But not Jodie Wallace. You already promised me you'd keep her away from me.'

Despite herself, Zara laughed.

'To be honest, when I arrived in Glengarrick, I had no intention of looking at anyone that way.'

She twisted a curl around her finger. Now was probably the time to tell him the last person she'd kissed was a woman. No doubt that would have him running for the hills. But a part of her didn't want to push him away. He was kind and sweet and had a great sense of humour. She liked him. And if nothing came of tonight other than one kiss in the middle of a packed dance floor because they'd been caught up in the mood and the music, then so be it.

But what if there *was* something in it? She would never know if she didn't give him a chance to get to know her. She shivered and when Ryan opened his arms for a hug, she let herself be drawn into the warmth of his chest.

'Zara, I know this is going to sound crazy, but I've wanted to kiss you since I first met you.'

She twisted in his arms to look up at him. 'Really?'

He nodded. 'After you'd given birth and you were holding Finn in your arms, I just wanted to hold both of you and kiss you and tell you how wonderful you were.'

She stared at him.

'Yeah, I know. Admitting that probably totally breaks your trust in me as a medical professional, but for a moment, watching you watching Finn, I forgot I was a doctor. All I saw was your strength and bravery.'

'And here I was, embarrassed that you'd seen me at my very worst.'

'I saw you at your best. The moment you became a mother.'

Zara's heart did another flip flop. This man knew all the right things to say. Others might argue they were just words, but she heard the sincerity in them and there was no denying the look of admiration on his face.

He tilted her chin and gently kissed her on the lips.

She smiled.

'Why are you smiling?'

'Because I've wanted to kiss you since you pulled up in my driveway on Thursday night and that's just weird because I don't remember the last time I had that type of visceral response to a man.'

'Not even to Finn's dad?'

She stiffened, wishing he hadn't asked, but knowing it was only fair he'd want to know about Finn's father. 'That's a whole other story.'

He reached for her hands and held them as he looked deep into her eyes. 'I hope it's a story you'll share with me one day soon.'

She licked her lips and gave a tiny nod. It was too soon to promise him anything, but if anything serious developed between them, she'd tell Ryan the whole story and hope he understood.

He stroked her cheek. 'I admire your courage, Zara, but it's more than that. I know we've only shared one sunset and one kiss, but I'm very drawn to you. This attraction has taken me by surprise, but something tells me these feelings aren't one-sided.'

Butterflies danced in her stomach. 'Definitely not one-sided.'

'Then I'd suggest we should become better acquainted.'

She laughed at his words and at the earnest expression on his face. She found herself nodding again even though thoughts were flying through her head. She had so much baggage she wasn't sure he'd still be interested in her after she told him everything.

Taking a step closer, he cradled her face between his hands. 'I really want to kiss you again if that's alright.'

It was more than alright. She wanted to do more than kiss him, but for now, this was enough.

His lips hovered above hers, waiting.

'It'll be better this time without an audience,' she said softly.

His lips brushed against hers then their breaths mingled just for an instant before she tasted him again. The urgency of the dance floor first kiss was gone, replaced with a slow tease that made her relax in his arms. His soft sighs stirred her blood and she forgot how cold she was. He kissed her and as he stroked her cheek her pulse skittered. When he lifted his mouth after a few moments to drag in a deep breath, she was a bit more disorientated than she preferred to admit.

She blinked rapidly as they separated. 'As much as I could do more of this, now's not the time. I need to get back inside before one of the girls comes looking for me.'

His eyes shone with need, and the urge to pull him into her arms and kiss him again was so strong Zara had to force herself to shove her cold hands in her pockets. When she stepped away from him, the loss of his warmth gave her a sharp stab of disappointment.

Chapter Thirteen

'If you stare any harder, you'll burn holes in him,' Georgie commented quietly when Zara was back at the table. Annabel and Emma were on the dance floor. 'He knows who you are, doesn't he?'

'Of course, he does. I was the one who didn't recognise him at first.' Zara grimaced as she tore her eyes off Ryan and back to her friend. 'I know I should stop looking at him and I keep telling myself not to, yet I keep doing it.'

'What happened between you two outside?' Georgie prodded, before taking a sip of her drink.

'You saw me leave with him?'

'Zazu, I'm your best friend. I've been watching you stare at him all night. And you can bet I saw that kiss on the dance floor too. I saw you leave and I watched him follow you.'

Zara glanced down at the timber tabletop and traced her finger along the worn grooves. 'We kissed again outside too,' she admitted softly. 'To be honest, I don't know what came over me or what I was thinking. I mean he doesn't know anything about me.'

'Does he need to just yet?' Georgie asked.

Zara sighed softly. 'He told me he'd like to take things further.'

Georgie beamed. 'That's a good thing, right?'

'It is. But if we go down that road, I have to be honest with him.' She looked up and met Georgie's steady gaze. 'About everything.'

'He already knows you have Finn. And that you've had breast cancer. At least those big hurdles are out of the way.'

'Yeah, but how will he feel when I tell him I can't have any more children?'

'I think you're probably jumping a bit far forward,' Georgie said.

'But if this—whatever *this* is—is going to go somewhere, I have to be upfront. Ryan has to know everything about my past. And I can't imagine he'll get past the gay thing.'

Georgie put her hand over Zara's. 'You don't know that.'

Silence fell and stretched.

'Like I said, don't overthink things, Zars. The kind of stuff you need to tell Ryan isn't the sort you talk about on a first date. He has to earn your trust. When it's right to tell him everything, you'll know.'

'You're right. As usual, I'm ten steps ahead of myself.'

'What was it like?' Georgie asked. 'Kissing him, I mean.'

'Good. Great. Amazing.' Zara's skin tingled at the memory of his kisses, but a flicker of doubt quickly followed. 'I shouldn't have kissed him in the first place. It wasn't the best idea I've ever had.'

'Why?'

'A million reasons. He's a paying guest. He's our town's new doctor. And I don't need to remind you this is a small town. You know how fast news spreads. Can you imagine what Mum will be like if she hears about me kissing a guy?'

Georgie chuckled. 'She'll be thrilled.'

'Yeah, well he's only here for the year so it's risky getting involved. Not just for myself but for Finn too. If he becomes attached to Ryan, he'll be broken hearted when Ryan returns to Queensland. That's where all his family is from. I can't imagine what would keep him in country Victoria.'

'Cross that bridge later. Do you like him?'

'Yeah, I do. I wouldn't have thought he was my type…but what do I know?'

This time Georgie laughed loudly. 'Do you actually have a type? She leaned in and put her elbows on the table. 'I'd suggest you stop over analysing things and just take each day as it comes. Enjoy the ride for a change. Remember what you were like before cancer? Zazu—life of the party. The one we always had to rein back in because she had crazy harebrained ideas.' She squeezed Zara's wrists. 'Find that girl again okay? We miss her.'

Tears formed in Zara's eyes and her throat threatened to close over. 'Oh, George. Maybe I should just forget this nonsense, get my head back on properly and stop drooling over a man who I can't possibly have a long-term future with.' She sat back in her chair and nibbled on a nail. 'Do you think anyone else saw us kissing?'

'Does it matter?' Georgie asked, giving her a pointed look. 'Kissing someone isn't a crime.'

'It's bigger than a crime in Glengarrick. You know how fast small-town gossip spreads. People love to talk.' The idea of becoming the topic of conversation again was too much. As much as the support she'd received from locals had been overwhelming at times, she didn't always want her business to be on everyone's lips.

'I think most people were too busy having a good time on the dance floor to notice.'

'But you noticed.'

'Because you're my best friend!'

'Fair.'

'Like I said, Zars, you are way overthinking this. I doubt anyone noticed. And even if they did, these people are your friends. They've stood by you with Finn and with the cancer. They might not gossip, but they sure as heck won't judge you. They'll be the first ones cheering you along. God knows you deserve happiness, and I can't think of a single person who would stand in your way.'

Deep down Zara knew that was true and that it was just her own overactive brain tormenting her as always.

Movement caught her eye across the room, and when she looked over, Ryan and his friends were getting ready to leave. She glanced at her watch, surprised that it was only eleven o'clock. Then she looked at Hamish and the poor guy could hardly stand up. It was probably just as well Ryan was taking him home.

Ryan glanced her way and when their eyes locked, a jolt of something hot and unspoken passed between them, leaving her weak and breathless again. He gave a small nod, before turning and walking out of the bar. That brief exchange had her heart galloping, and her palms damp.

Once Ryan was gone, Zara couldn't think of any reason to stay. It was as if, for her, the night was over, and it was time to go home.

She pressed a hand to her cheek. 'That champagne went straight to my head.'

Georgie laughed. 'I reckon the only thing that's gone to your head is Dr Delicious.'

Zara laughed and shook her head. 'No. It was definitely the alcohol.'

'You keep telling yourself that, honey, if that's what it takes.'

It was nearly midnight by the time Zara had dropped the others home and was driving back to the farm. She was exhausted, but also buzzing, reliving Ryan's kisses on a loop in her mind and wondering what tomorrow would bring when she saw him again.

Chapter Fourteen

Hamish was passed out in the front seat, so drunk he'd hardly been able to walk from the pub to the car. Ryan smirked. His mates were going to have hell of hangovers in the morning.

Back at Braxton Park, Ryan pulled up in front of the cottage Hamish and Rob were sharing. Dan got out of the car too and he and Rob helped Hamish inside. Ryan followed them.

'I might as well sleep on the couch here tonight,' Dan told Ryan. 'That way you won't wake me in the morning. And I won't keep you up with my snoring.'

'Doesn't bother me,' Ryan said. 'I can sleep through anything. And that couch won't be comfortable.'

But Dan already had his shoes off and had flopped onto the couch.

'I take it riding's off the agenda for you guys tomorrow,' Ryan said as he helped get Hamish's shoes off and steered him towards the bedroom.

Hamish groaned. 'I think everything's off the agenda. Why did you let me drink so much?'

'It's your buck's party.'

After Ryan said goodnight to his friends, rather than drive the fifty metres back to his cottage, he walked. The sky was inky black, and the stars were like diamonds glittering above his head. He looked up at Zara's house. The lights were out except for one at the back, which he presumed was Zara's bedroom. Was she home yet? He thrust his hands in his jeans pockets and slowed his stride. It was cold, but he was in no hurry to go back inside. Maybe the fresh cold night air would clear his muddled head.

From the moment he'd seen Zara again on Thursday, he hadn't been able to stop thinking about her. Now he'd tasted her sweetness and held her in his arms, there wasn't a chance he was going to be able to sleep. At least not without taking a cold shower. It had been hard enough stopping at kissing her tonight.

Not wanting to call it a night, he did a loop, passing the stables, the house and walking past the other cabins, until he got to his. Instead of going inside, he sank down on the steps and let out his breath slowly.

He was only there a moment, with the sound of crickets and the stars shining bright above him, when he heard movement from inside the cottage behind him.

He stilled and cocked his head, listening intently for any more sounds. Nothing. Maybe he'd imagined it. Still, he eased slowly to his feet and stealthily made his way to the door. It should've been locked, but a slow turn of the knob had the door swinging inwards. In the dim light he could see a man in a hoodie sitting on the couch. On his lap was Ryan's open laptop. As soon as Ryan shouted, the guy leapt to his feet and bolted out the back door, abandoning the computer where he tossed it.

Ryan sprinted after him, shouting at him to stop. Anger and adrenaline gave him the extra kick he needed to catch up to the man. He grabbed him by the hood of his jumper and jerked him to a stop before throwing him to the ground. When he swung him around, the moonlight briefly illuminated his features and Ryan looked down in disbelief. He was only a kid. Lucky if he was thirteen.

Before he'd got over his shock, headlights bounced up the drive, lighting them up in its beams. Zara's car came to a stop and she jumped out, leaving the passenger door open. She ran over to them.

'What's going on?' she yelled.

In Ryan's grip, the teen trembled. 'I found this kid in my cottage. He was trying to steal my laptop.'

Zara leaned closer to the teenager and gasped. 'Andy Goddard?'

He mumbled something in reply and dropped his head.

'Your father is going to tear strips off you. What the hell were you thinking stealing Ryan's laptop?'

'I wasn't trying to steal it.' Despite his obvious fear, his words were defiant.

'I'd say if you broke into one of my cottages and grabbed a guest's computer, it sure sounds like stealing to me,' Zara said, voice steely. Ryan had a quick image flash through his mind of Zara standing up in court and staring down a witness. If she was like this, she'd be formidable.

Andy kept his eyes fixed on the ground.

'Ryan, are you okay?' Zara asked, turned to him. 'Did he take anything else?'

'I'm fine. And I have no idea. I just walked in and saw him on my laptop.'

'Right.' Zara pulled her phone out brought it to her ear.

She stepped away and Ryan kept his attention on the kid, but he heard enough to figure she was speaking to someone at the police station.

When she finished her call, Zara came to a stop beside them, folding her arms across her chest. Ryan exhaled loudly. The last thing he wanted was to make a scene. He'd left Queensland and taken this job in Victoria to get away from the drama. He shook his head, trying to clear it. If this kid had wanted to steal Ryan's laptop, he would have taken it and run instead of dropping it on the couch. What the hell had he been doing? And how had he logged on? After everything that had happened with Malinda, Ryan was fastidious about passwords and security.

'What were you doing on my laptop?' he asked.

Andy didn't reply.

'Andy?' Zara prodded. 'What were you doing on Dr Dunlop's computer?'

He shrugged. 'I heard he was staying here and one of the guys told me if I could figure out how to log on, I'd be able to do those e-scripts.'

Ryan exhaled loudly. 'Drugs.'

'They're not for me,' Andy said, in a whining voice. 'I don't do drugs.'

'But you're happy to deal them,' Zara said. She turned to Ryan. 'Why don't we all go inside? It's late and it's cold. The police will be here in about fifteen minutes. I'll put the kettle on and we can get to the bottom of all this.'

Ryan followed Zara inside, his hand on the kid's hoodie in case he tried to bolt.

'Want to tell me what you were thinking, Andy?' Zara was the first to break the silence after she'd made cups of tea for herself and Ryan and a hot chocolate for Andy.

'I'm in trouble, aren't I?' Andy asked.

'It depends,' Ryan replied. If this kid was charged, it would change his entire life. He glanced at Zara. Her face was difficult to read. She looked angry, but he wasn't sure if it was at Andy, Ryan or the situation.

While they waited for the police to arrive, Ryan and Zara worked hard to engage Andy in conversation. It turned out he had a reputation for being good with computers. A couple of older kids from school had approached him and offered to pay him money if he hacked into Ryan's computer and got the scripts they wanted. When Andy refused, they threatened to hurt his little sister. He hadn't felt he had any option. It wasn't drugs Andy wanted. He wanted to protect his sister. And the money had been appealing too.

As his story came out, Ryan felt sorry for him. He wasn't a bad kid at, just a scared one.

The best thing would be to find him a job so he could earn money legitimately and keep out of trouble.

As they spoke, an idea formed. When Zara got up to take their empty cups back to the kitchen, he followed her.

'I'm so sorry Ryan. This never should have happened.'

'It's not your fault.'

'Was anything else taken?' she asked.

'I haven't checked, but I doubt it.'

'He's not a bad kid.'

'I agree. But he's easily led and I think if you're interested, we can help him and make sure he's kept on the right track.'

She frowned. 'How?'

'Horse therapy.'

'What?'

'Have you heard of equine assisted therapy?'

'Of course. But I'm not in a position to run any type of program.'

'I'm not suggesting you need to formalise anything. But you could use help with the horses—feeding them, taking off rugs, picking up poo. No reason Andy couldn't do that. Let the horses lead the way and they'll build a connection with Andy without him realising.'

'I guess so.'

'You wouldn't have to pay him much.' A thought raced through him and he mentally slapped his head. 'Sorry. That's very high handed of me. I'm presuming you're in a position to pay the kid some money. If you're not, I'd be happy to help.'

She shook her head. 'No, I could afford to pay him a few hours a week.'

'And of course, I have no idea if his parents would be happy to drive him out here.'

'His dad would. I'll speak to him and tell them what happened.'

*

It was nearly twelve-thirty when headlights beamed down the drive.

A couple of moments passed before there was a knock on the door. Before Zara had a chance to get up to open it, a man entered.

'Good evening everyone.' He went straight to Zara and gave her a hug. 'Are you okay, Zars?' he asked softly.

She nodded as she hugged him back. 'I'm fine.'

He turned and moved towards Ryan, hand outstretched. 'Dr Dunlop. Heard all about you. I'm Senior Sergeant Ben Mitchell.'

Ryan felt a wave of heat steal up the back of his neck. Great. The cop clearly knew all about his history which meant everyone in town probably did too. How was that going to affect his job? He pushed the concerns aside and smiled as he shook Ben's hand. 'Call me Ryan.'

'What's the trouble?' Ben asked.

'It's Andy,' Zara said, stepping in between the two men. 'He was trying to steal e-scripts off Ryan's laptop.'

Ben looked from Andy to Ryan. 'Did Andy break into your cottage?'

'I probably left the door unlocked. So, no, technically he didn't break in.'

Ben frowned. 'I know we're in the country, but it doesn't seem a very wise idea to leave your door unlocked and your laptop lying around if it gives access to anyone to write prescriptions.'

'What Andy would have realised very quickly is that this laptop is my personal one and I don't have any medical software on it,' Ryan replied evenly.

'Do you want to press charges?' Ben asked.

'No, I don't.'

Andy's head snapped up and his eyes widened in surprise. 'You don't?'

'Zara? What about you? It's your property,' Ben asked.

She shook her head. 'No. I'd like to offer Andy a deal instead.'

'What kind of deal?' Andy's eyes darted from adult to adult.

'How would you like a job? It won't pay much, but it will be a start. It shouldn't take long for you to save up for that computer you want.'

'Doing what?'

'Helping with the horses.'

'But I don't like horses. Plus, I'm probably allergic.'

Ryan chuckled. 'Then lucky I'm a doctor and I can tell you which antihistamine to buy.'

'If you don't like horses, I'm sure I can arrange for you to volunteer somewhere else. Maybe at the aged care home,' Zara said.

'Uh-uh. No way.'

'Good. That's settled then. I'll speak to your dad.'

'Zars, can I chat to you for a second?' Ben asked, putting his hand on Zara's shoulder.

Surprised at the affectionate gesture and familiarity of using her nickname, Ryan tensed as Ben led Zara into the kitchen, just out of earshot. He watched the two of them through narrowed eyes, trying to ignore the flicker of jealousy as he strained to hear what they were saying. He read the concern on Ben's face but when he pulled Zara into a tender hug and brushed a kiss across the top of her head, Ryan turned away. There was clearly history here, something deeper than just two people who knew each other. An ex-boyfriend perhaps?

Ben returned and faced Andy. 'Do we have a deal, or would you prefer to face court?'

'Fine.'

'Sorry, I didn't hear you.'

Andy groaned and stubbed his sneaker into the carpet.

'Do you have a problem with something?' Ben asked. 'Because I can ignore what Zara and Dr Dunlop want and arrest you.'

Zara stepped forward and put her hand on Ben's arm. 'It'll be fine, Ben.' She flashed him a bright smile.

'Alright. But you're allowed to change your mind.' Ben turned to Andy. 'How about I drive you back home. I presume you have your bike here.'

Andy dipped his head. 'No, one of the guys dropped me at the front gate and I walked.'

'I'll be wanting the names of those guys at some point too, Andy.'

His eyes widened. 'They'll kill me for dobbing on them and I don't want them to hurt my sister.'

'Guess you should have thought about that before getting involved with them. Come on.'

At the front door, Ben put his arm around Zara's shoulders and gave her a sideways hug. 'I'll see you on tomorrow when you drop Finn off. Around nine?'

Zara nodded. 'Or later if it suits. He's staying at Mum and Dad's tonight. I'll pick him after mid-morning then drop him to yours.'

After they were gone, Ryan turned to Zara, and using every ounce of control, calmly asked, 'What's the deal with you two?'

Chapter Fifteen

Zara wince at Ryan's question. How much should she tell him? How would he react?

She stared at him, searching for words, silence descending on the house. Ryan moved to look out of the window. He exhaled loudly and when he turned a muscle worked in his jaw briefly before his expression softened.

Zara realised what he must be thinking. Sure, they'd only shared a kiss and weren't even officially dating, but she already felt an emotional connection with him. The urge to confide in him and trust him with her secrets was strong even though a part of her was terrified he'd walk away before they'd even had a chance to take their relationship further. But she had to try.

She went to the couch, sat down, and patted the seat beside her. 'I know it's late and we're both tired, but I don't want you to leave without me explaining to you my relationship with Ben.

Ryan looked at her for a moment. 'Alright,' he said, and joined her on the couch.

'Ben is my best friend,' she said, pulling a cushion into her lap and hugging it to her chest. 'We've been friends since before we could talk.' It probably looked more than that to Ryan but if they were going to build a relationship, he needed to know from the outset that Ben was a big part of her life.

Ryan nodded. 'I have to admit, I was a bit surprised when he hugged you like that. Not that you're not allowed to hug other guys,' he rushed on, 'but for a second I thought the two of you were a couple.'

'Definitely not. And I'm sorry you thought that.' She released the cushion and put a hand on his thigh. 'You couldn't be more wrong. Ben is very happily married to Annabel.'

Ryan exhaled loudly and a look of relief crossed his face. 'He cares deeply about you. That much is obvious.'

'And I care about him,' she said. 'Ben has been by my side for a lot of my life, especially during the last two years while I've raised Finn on my own and of course he was there while I fought cancer.'

Ryan's expression softened further. He took the cushion from her grasp, took her hands in his and squeezed them gently. 'You're amazing, do you know that?'

His quiet declaration strengthened her feelings for him further, and a lump grew in her throat. She shook her head, 'I'm not. I just have amazing people in my life.'

'Don't put yourself down. I think you're incredible. I told you, that moment after you gave birth, I thought you were the strongest person I'd met.' He touched her cheek. 'I still think that.'

It had been a long time since anyone had looked at her the way Ryan was, let alone tell her they thought she was special. Tears pooled in her eyes and she blinked them away.

'Thank you.' She wanted to tell him more, but now didn't seem the right time. 'I think what you suggested for Andy is a good idea.'

He seemed momentarily thrown off-balance by the change of topic.

'I didn't think he should be allowed to walk away without consequences. This might teach him not to do anything like this again.'

She nodded.

'Will you speak to his parents?'

'To his dad. His mum walked out a few years ago—couldn't cope living on the farm. She left the kids behind. Andy's dad's a good guy. He'll support what's best for Andy.'

He ran his hands through his beard. 'I hope you don't mind me suggesting it.'

'Not at all. If I didn't want to, I would have said so. I think your idea has some merit. I'll need to do some research, but the farm is big enough for lots more horses. Maybe I could put out some feelers and see if anyone is interested in running an equine therapy program out here. I have a friend who is a psychologist and loves horses. I'll have a chat to him and see if we can pull something together.'

'You'd have a dozen referrals before you even opened, I'm sure.'

She yawned, and even though she quickly covered her mouth with her hand, Ryan noticed.

'God, Zara, it's after one. I hadn't realised how late it is. We should get to bed.'

'We?'

He arched his brows at her. 'Don't tempt me. *You* need to go to bed.' He chuckled. 'And I need to take a very cool shower.'

He moved closer and tucked a stray strand of hair behind her ear, her pulse quickening further at the tenderness of his simple gesture.

She stifled a yawn. 'It would be nice to sit up and talk until the sun comes up, but I have to pick up Finn from my parents in the morning and trust me, chasing after Finn on no sleep would not be good.'

Ryan stood and helped her to her feet. 'Why don't we have breakfast together? Come down to the cottage and I'll cook. The incredible woman who runs this place left the fridge full of breakfast ingredients.'

She chuckled. 'I'd like that.'

'It will give us a chance to talk about us.'

Her heart thudded in her ears. 'Is there an "us"?' she asked softly.

'That depends.'

'On what?'

'On what you want.'

I want to kiss you again. 'I'm not sure what I want, to be honest. This is all so new and unexpected. Plus, I have a lot to consider, including Finn.'

'I can tell you what I want.'

She stared at him.

'I want more of you.'

She tipped her head to one side. 'Are you flirting with me, Dr Dunlop? Because if you are, that line was dreadful.'

He chuckled. 'Is this classified as flirting? I have no idea. It's been a long time and I'm a bit rusty.'

She yawned properly this time. 'To be honest, right now I'm too tired to think. It's been a big day and all I know is we have another big day planned tomorrow.' As she was speaking, her head whirred with how much she had to do. 'Maybe we could skip breakfast so we can get a sleep in. As much as I'd like to, I need to pick up Finn then drop him off at Ben and Annabel's. They're looking after him so I can take you guys riding.'

'Ah, about that. I don't think the guys are keen. I reckon they'll be passed out until at least noon, then they'll wander down to the river and go fishing.'

Disappointment went through her. She'd been looking forward to the horse ride.

'But you and I could still go if you like.'

When Ryan smiled at her like that, it melted her heart all over again. Even if she hadn't been utterly exhausted, it would be hard to think straight with him being so nearby.

'I'd love that,' she replied.

He touched her cheek gently. 'Just you and I and a leisurely ride. I can't think of a better way to spend time.'

'Neither can I. Sorry about breakfast though. It was a great idea, but the timing isn't right.'

'Plenty of time for breakfasts together in our future.'

His voice was husky, and she couldn't make her legs move to take a step away. Was he thinking about their kiss again? Because she certainly was.

'I hope so,' she said with a smile.

He broke eye contact first and headed for the front door, then paused with his hand on the doorknob. 'Goodnight, Zara. If I kiss you now, they'll be no sleeping for either of us tonight. I'll see you tomorrow.'

He opened the door, slipped out, and with a wave and a smile he was gone.

Chapter Sixteen

After a restless night, with her head filled with thoughts of Ryan, Zara got up as dawn was starting to lighten the sky and headed out for an early morning ride on Colby, her retired racehorse. Even though she and Ryan were going to ride later, she wanted a chance to be on her own to think. And there was no better place to think than on the back of a horse. It was her place of refuge. She didn't often get to ride in the mornings, but every time her parents took Finn overnight, she grabbed the chance.

The forecast was for another chilly day with a chance of snow in the mountains. As she cantered along the sandy sheep track that threaded its way through the property, the morning fog was just starting to lift, and the green grass in the paddocks sparkled with dew. On either side of the path huge gum trees towered, their leaves casting dappled shadows on the ground.

All night thoughts had crowded in, piling on top of the same old broken records in her head. She still had a lot of emotional baggage to sort through, and she wasn't sure if she was ready for a relationship yet. Even with a guy as great as Ryan.

Not only had she lain awake thinking about kissing Ryan, but she'd been thinking about her offer of letting him rent out the cottage for twelve months. It made financial sense to her. Having him in the cottage at a lower rate was still better than only having fifty percent occupancy.

She also hadn't been able to stop thinking about his suggestion of running an equine assisted therapy program at the farm. It was a great idea, and she couldn't wait to do some research on it. She had the room, and she had the horses. All she would need would be someone who had the expertise as a psychologist or counsellor.

It was nearly nine o'clock when Zara pulled Colby up and let the reins hang loose on his neck, slowing her breathing and letting her horse catch his. She scratched his wither. He was such a good horse.

As she walked him back to the stables, she looked around and inhaled deeply, her nostrils filling with the smell of woodsmoke coming from one of the cottages. She looked across at them. Ryan was up but there didn't appear to be any movement at the other cottage. No doubt the other men were sleeping off their late night at the pub.

She was in the stables brushing Colby when she heard footsteps on gravel.

'Good morning.'

Ryan's deep voice caused butterflies to dance in her stomach and when he leaned on the stable door, she caught a waft of his aftershave and felt suddenly lightheaded.

'Hi.'

Ryan was dressed for the wintry weather, looking like he'd stepped out of an R.M. Williams catalogue in his jeans, plaid flannel shirt and boots. The only thing that didn't match the quintessential country look was the blue and white Geelong Cats beanie on his head.

She pointed to it. 'What's with that? I thought you worked for the Suns?'

'I did. But Geelong has been my team since I was a kid.'

'That'll make Jed happy.'

'What about you? Who do you follow?'

'Melbourne.'

'Ah, the Dees. Been a while since they won a premiership.'

She chuckled. 'Don't remind me.'

He rubbed Colby's blaze. 'You went riding without me.'

'I couldn't sleep, and I figured I'd take Colby out early. We'll still ride later but I'll take a different horse.'

'Good. I'm looking forward to it.' He smiled. 'Sorry to hear you couldn't sleep though. Would it make you feel any better to know my dreams were of you?'

She ducked under Colby's neck to hide the flush that had crept up her neck and brushed the other side of him, removing the sweat patches from where his saddle had sat. Every inch of her was aware of Ryan's presence.

Not usually the self-conscious type, she now swam in the sensation. Last night at the pub Ryan had seen her at her best. Dressed up to the nines and playing up her looks. Today she was back to her normal self. No makeup, no nice clothes, no fancy hair. Just her riding clothes and a puffer jacket that did more to hide her curves than accentuate them. She wasn't plain, but there wasn't anything about her looks right now that should attract attention. Nothing like the kind of women in Ryan's social media feed.

When she couldn't sleep last night, she'd stalked him. None of the pictures were current, but if she believed the photos on Facebook, it showed she was not his type. Then again, she was usually a good judge of character and she felt like she knew him well enough already to know there was nothing shallow or superficial about him.

'I have to head into town soon to pick up Finn from Mum and Dad's and take him to Ben's. Would you like to come with me? We could grab a coffee at The Silver Spoon.'

'Sold. I appreciate the coffee machine in the cottage, but it's never the same, or as good, as one made by someone else.'

'Okay. Let me put finish brushing Colby, then I'll put him back in his paddock. Once I'm sorted here, I'll get changed and we can go into town. Does that suit you?'

'Perfectly. Are you happy for me to have a wander around and check out the horses?'

'Absolutely. Make yourself at home.'

'Speaking of which, we should talk about your offer of me staying long term in the cottage.'

'Yes, we should do that.'

Once she was satisfied the horses were happy, she headed back to the house with Ryan keeping step beside her. She pushed open the back door. 'Come in. Make yourself at home. I'll go and get changed, then we can head into town.'

By the time they were in her car and heading into town, a misty rain had started falling.

'I hope it clears up,' Ryan said, peering out the front windscreen. 'It would be a shame to cancel the ride.'

'A little bit of rain doesn't hurt. I have a Drizabone you can borrow.'

'Perfect.'

Chapter Seventeen

For the next ten minutes on the drive into Glengarrick, neither of them struggled for conversation as they chatted about all sorts of things, finding out how much they had in common.

The main street was slowly coming to life, typical for this time on a Sunday morning. Zara parked at one end of the main street so they could walk down it towards The Silver Spoon.

They got out of the car and the smell of fresh bread, pastries and coffee wafted down the street, making Zara's stomach growl. Or maybe her stomach was churning because she was acutely aware of the handsome man next to her.

The low clouds out at the farm that had formed a veil of mist were starting to lift in town, but it was still cold. At the top of the main street Zara pulled up the collar of her coat and wrapped her scarf tighter to ward off the chill.

When Ryan took her hand in his, it sent a ripple of pleasure and warmth through her and although a split second of self-doubt also went through her, she squeezed his fingers in return. They made their way down the street slowly, neither of them in a hurry.

One of the checkout girls was putting up the week's specials on the board outside the IGA supermarket and she waved and grinned as they walked past. Another teenager rolled a rack of clothes from the sporting goods store onto the footpath and propped sandbags on the rack to stop it rolling away. The mannequins in the window were dressed in Glengarrick football club colours.

Jonesy, the old guy who ran the service station, gave Zara a wave and a curious look, as did Sue, the woman sweeping the footpath in front of the tourist information centre. Zara kept her head high and didn't let go of Ryan's hand even though she could just imagine what everyone was thinking. If anyone had seen them kissing last night at the pub, the news would be around town by now. By holding his hand, she might as well have a sign over her head saying "yes, this is him".

To keep her mind where it should be, Zara kept up a commentary for Ryan about the different people and shops in the main street. Over the road from the bakery, the Italian pizzeria was dark.

'By six o'clock tonight it will be packed, and they'll have people lining up out the door to collect their take away orders.' Next to the pizza place was the fish and chip shop. 'That's been owned by three generations of the Kalogeras family. Trust me, they make the best souvlakis you'll ever taste.'

'I'm sure I'll become a regular,' Ryan replied.

'You will. Trust me.'

On the opposite side of the road was the Main Street Café. 'That's where the oldies gather,' she said, pointing it out. 'If you're ever looking for your elderly patients, you'll find them there enjoying a chat over a pot of tea and coffee scrolls or scones with jam and cream. The owners are lovely people and I think it's fabulous the way they cater for the seniors in town. Some of them find Georgie's café's a bit loud.'

They crossed the road and walked another fifty metres to the café. Once inside, Zara led him to a small table in the corner near a window. She waved at Georgie behind the counter and her best friend grinned and waved back.

Once they were seated, Ryan tried to catch her hands in his again. She gently eased her fingers from his. 'I'm not worried about what people will say. I just feel a bit self-conscious. No-one will judge me, but they're likely to ask lots of questions. And I know my best friend. She'll tease me unrelentingly if she thinks we're an item already.'

Understanding crossed his face. 'Of course,' he said, letting go of her hands. 'Sorry. I don't want to make you uncomfortable.'

Georgie appeared at their table with menus and a hug for Zara.

'Ryan, you remember my best friend Georgie.'

'I do. Good to see you again.'

'Great to see you too, Ryan. I hear you're our new doctor. I hope Zara's told you we're like one big family here in Glengarrick. It'll be great having you part of our community.' She grinned. 'I don't think you'll struggle to get patients.'

Ryan smiled back. 'I hope not. I was worried some of the older folk would be used to Laura and might not be pleased with a new doctor.'

'Oh, trust me, they won't mind at all. Now, what would you like to eat?'

'We're just here for a coffee,' Zara said. 'I've already eaten.'

Ryan looked at her. 'Do you mind if I have something? If we have time that is.'

She checked her phone. 'I guess we're not in a hurry.'

Ryan smiled up at Georgie. 'I'll have whatever you recommend.'

'The Big Breakfast it is. And a coffee of course.'

'Naturally. A latte would be great.'

Zara relaxed as she watched Ryan chat easily with her best friend. She liked that about him—that he had the ability to talk to anyone and make other people feel comfortable around him.

She touched his arm. 'Remember we're still going riding when we get home. You'd better not fill up on too much food or you might struggle to get into the saddle.'

'I'm sure I'll be fine.' He smiled from Zara to Georgie. 'Make that latte a large one please.'

Georgie grinned. 'Coming right up.' She turned to Zara. 'I'll bring you a muffin.'

Zara groaned. 'Your baking will make me fat.'

'Rubbish.'

After Georgie left, Ryan leaned in, resting his elbows on the table. 'Let's talk about your offer of the cottage. Does it still stand? Because I don't want you to feel pressured. My plan was to head into town on Monday and see if there are any vacant properties. I can always stay at your parent's pub in the meantime.'

She shook her head. 'You don't want to do that. You need your own space, not just a room. When I first decided to move back to Glengarrick when I was pregnant with Finn, I stayed with my parents for a bit until Braxton Park came on the market and I snapped it up. Such a good decision. Anyway, I was thinking we could move some of the furniture out of the cottage so you can move your own things in. I assume you're going back to Queensland first to pick up your stuff.'

'No. I don't need to. I left it all there. I've rented out my place on the Gold Coast fully furnished. It was easier that way. It would have cost a bomb to have everything put in storage then trucked down here. Hardly worth it for a year.'

'So you'd like me to leave the furniture in the cottage?'

'If you don't mind, I'd love it if you left everything. The cottage is perfect.'

'You're welcome to decorate it however you like.'

He chuckled. 'I'm a bloke, Zara. I don't care if there's no knickknacks or personal items. As long as there's a bed, a TV, a couch and enough equipment in the kitchen to make a meal, I'm happy. Honestly, I don't need much. Although we might have to work something out about the internet. The coverage down there is very patchy.'

'Of course. We'll get the phone company people to come and see what they can do.'

'Sounds good.'

She chewed her bottom lip. What if he thought her price was too high? She named a figure, and when he frowned, she screwed up her face.

'If that's too much, I'm happy to negotiate.'

'It's not too much at all. Surely that's too cheap.'

'No. I don't think so. I worked it out in my head last night. It'll be fine.'

'I'd like to get a proper contract drawn up.'

'That won't take long. I was a lawyer in a former life. I can draw up a contract with my eyes closed.'

His eyebrows shot up. 'You were?'

She smiled. 'There's lots about me you don't know.'

'Yet.'

Georgie appeared with their coffees.

After they'd both taken a sip, Zara licked her lips. Her mouth was dry just thinking about how to say what she wanted to say. She had no idea how, in such a short space of time, her feelings for Ryan had gone from a small ember to a full-blown flame, but they had. And she needed to talk that through with him. It was clear by the way he was looking at her that he wanted a relationship with her too, but she still had her concerns and wanted to voice them before they took things any further.

'Can we talk about what happened at the pub?' she asked.

'At the pub?' Ryan asked, feigning ignorance.

She rolled her eyes at him. 'The kiss.'

'Ah,' he drawled. 'The kiss. You want to talk about the kiss.'

'Yes, I do. That and what happens next.'

His face changed from teasing to serious. 'That's up to you, Zara. I don't want to push you, but I think—I hope—I'm making it clear. I'd really like to take the next step with you.'

She dipped her head and took another sip of her coffee. When she looked up, Ryan was watching her, waiting for her reply.

She swallowed and put her cup down. 'The thing is, Ryan, you're only here for a year, and like you said, it'll go quickly. Is it worth starting something we both know has an end date?'

'I think it is. I'm not sure how to put this properly without sounding like I'm rushing into things and pushing you, but if this relationship goes where I'd like it to go, I'm more than happy to investigate work locally on a permanent basis. It might not be in Glengarrick, but I'm sure there are always positions at the hospital in Stockton. I don't have to work as a GP.'

She let out her breath slowly. Was she ready to make the leap into a relationship this quickly? It felt right, but she'd been known in the past to jump into things without looking at the dangers below.

'Tell me I'm wrong, Zara. Tell me you're perfectly happy being single, and I'll walk away.'

He took her hands again and this time she let him.

'Zara.'

There was a plea in his words, and the look in his eyes made her heart pound and her stomach tighten.

'If I'm wrong about this, then tell me. Say the words, and we can just be friends.'

'You're not wrong,' she whispered. 'I want to take this further.'

'But?'

'But Glengarrick is a small town. There are no secrets here. I can almost guarantee by this afternoon ten people will mention they saw us together and just like that,' she let go of one hand and clicked her fingers, 'we'll be an item.'

'Is that so bad?'

She lifted a shoulder and let it drop. 'Probably not.'

'They might talk about us but we're both consenting adults. We don't have anything to prove by getting caught up in gossip. If you want to go out with me, you can. If you want to sleep with me, you can do that too and you don't have to answer to anyone.'

Her mouth dropped open. She leaned in and lowered her voice. 'How did we just jump from kissing to sex?'

'I don't know, but I'm happy to try.'

He grinned then squeezed her hands and his laugh was warm and easy, and it lessened the tension in her shoulders.

'I'm joking, Zara. We can take things at your pace. We have Finn to think about too. I want to be sure we know where he fits into this picture.'

'The problem is I've known these people my entire life. Over the past two years they've become mine and Finn's family. They'll be looking out for us and I know they'll have questions. Actually, they'll have opinions. Lots of opinions. It won't be easy for either of us. I don't want to put you in a position where they're bothering you at work.'

Ryan sat back in his chair. 'You want to know what's not easy?'

She looked him in the eye and saw a flicker of desire.

He leaned back in and rubbed the back of her hands with his thumbs. 'What's not easy, Zara Pritchard, is wanting you, and knowing you might not want me.'

She frowned. 'Why wouldn't I want you?'

'I come with a lot of baggage.'

'Baggage?' She rolled her eyes. 'Yeah, right. Well, just so you know, I've got suitcases of baggage. You have no idea.'

'Then we can unpack things and go on a journey together. What do you think? Why don't we just take things one day at a time and see what happens? Can you do that?'

She nodded. 'I think so.'

'You don't have to decide now, Zara,' he said gently. 'Just think about what I said. That's all I'm asking. Think about whether you want to walk away without knowing what it could be like between us.'

There it was again. The hunger in his eyes.

She swallowed and lifted her chin. 'I can try.'

Georgie returned to their table with impeccable timing and placed plates of food in front of them. She delivered them with a knowing look in Zara's direction. A look that was also filled with questions.

While they ate, conversation jumped from topic to topic and they chatted easily about a range of things, learning how much they had in common. As they were finishing, Zara's phone rang. She pulled it out of her bag and looked at it. It was Ben.

She glanced at Ryan. 'Sorry, I need to take this.'

'Go ahead. I'll go and pay.'

She reached for her wallet, but Ryan waved it away. 'You can pay next time.'

She put the phone to her ear. 'Hey. Sorry I got caught up. I haven't picked Finn up yet.'

'I know. I was going to offer to pick him up from your parents and save you the drive into town, but I've just driven down the main street and I saw your car. Where are you?'

'I'm at the café.'

'Do you want me to get Finn?'

'Are you sure you don't mind?'

'I offered, Zars.'

'Thanks, Ben. I feel like a bad mother.'

'Don't be silly. You're an awesome mum. I'll drop him home later this afternoon. What time do your guests check out?'

'Not until first thing tomorrow.' She decided now wasn't the time to tell Ben that Ryan was staying.

'If I come out around about four, or when he's woken up from his afternoon nap, will that suit?'

'That would be great. If he won't go to sleep for you, just bring him home and I can put him to bed earlier tonight.'

'We'll see how we go.'

'Thank you, Ben.'

There was a long pause.

'Hey, Zars, just take things slowly, okay?'

'What do you mean?'

'You and the doctor. Don't rush into anything.'

'Of course not. When have I ever rushed into anything?'

Ben chuckled. 'I'll see you later today.'

Chapter Eighteen

Hamish, Rob and Dan were awake when she and Ryan got back from town around eleven. Surprisingly they didn't appear to be too under the weather. They declined Zara's offer to go horse riding though, saying they wanted to spend the afternoon fishing. Ryan naturally opted to join them.

'If you're interested, I can prepare dinner for us,' Zara said. One of the things she liked to do was offer guests a meal. It added another element to the personal touch she prided herself in. Not a lot of people took up the option, not wanting to impose, but she hoped these guys would. She had an idea up her sleeve and this seemed the best way to make it happen.

'Are you sure?' Hamish asked. 'That would be great. Saves us driving back into town. Although the food at the pub is great.'

'Only if it's not too much work for you,' Ryan said.

'Not at all.' She smiled at him. 'I enjoy cooking.' She hesitated. She didn't want her next question to seem staged, even though it was part of her plan. 'Would it be okay if I invite a few of my friends over? The weather is perfect to sit around the firepit and I know you'll all get along. It doesn't have to be a late night. I know you're all checking out first thing in the morning.'

Hamish looked at the others and shrugged. 'Sounds good to me. More the merrier.'

After the guys had gone, Zara called Georgie. 'Hey. Are you guys doing anything for dinner tonight?'

'No. Why?'

'I'm going to put some legs of lamb into the oven for my guests. Just wondering if you want to come out and join us.'

There was a long stretch of silence over the phone.

Zara sighed. 'Oh okay, I want you and Jed to come and check Ryan out and tell me I'm not acting like a lovestruck teenager.'

Georgie chuckled. 'I watched how he looked at you today at the café. If anyone's lovestruck, it's Ryan. I think it's cute.'

'Yeah, well, you might think it's cute, but Ben reminded me today I have a habit of jumping into things without thinking.'

'That's what we love about you, Zars.'

'Well, this time I'm asking you to stop me if you think I'm making a big mistake. Just be subtle okay?'

'Too easy. I can do subtle. Not sure about Jed though. He'll probably ask Ryan all the hard questions. Anyway, I'll bring dessert. It'll be fun. Who else are you inviting?'

'I'll see if Ben and Annabel want to come too.'

'Good idea. Ben's a good judge of character. He'll tell you if he thinks you need to be careful.'

Zara was peeling potatoes when she heard Ben pull up. Moments later the door opened, and Finn burst into the kitchen. She put down the veggie peeler and scooped him into her arms.

'Hey buddy, did you have a good time?'

Finn wriggled out of her grip and darted off to his room.

'He's had a ball,' Ben said, dropping Finn's overnight bag on the floor. 'Although sorry, he didn't get much of a nap this afternoon.'

'That's okay. He can have an early night.'

'What are you cooking?' Ben said, stepping past her into the kitchen and opening the oven door. 'Wow. That's a lot of meat for two people.'

'Yeah, about that. Jed and Georgie are coming for dinner. Are you and Annabel free? I'm making dinner for the guys staying in the cottages too and I thought it would be great to get the fire going and hang out.'

Ben narrowed his gaze. 'You really like this doctor, don't you?'

She nodded. Despite the fact she'd only just met him, there was no question in her mind that if she opened her heart to Ryan and let him in, there was every chance he could be someone she could share the rest of her life with.

'I'm a little scared it's all happening too quickly,' she admitted. 'Not that I'm worried what people will say. I'm more worried I'm going into this blindly.'

'And you want us to check him out?'

She nodded again. 'As long as it doesn't appear that's what you're doing.'

'Leave it to me and Jed. By the end of the night, we'll let you know what kind of a bloke he is.'

'Just don't scare him off, okay?'

'I'll scare him off if he's not the right guy for you and Finn. Deal?'

'Yeah, deal.'

*

Zara smiled at Hamish as she cleared away the last of the dessert plates from the outdoor table. 'I hope you've had a lovely weekend.'

'It's been fabulous. Thank you. And thanks for this,' Hamish said, indicating the remnants of their lovely meal. 'It was really kind of you.'

'My pleasure.' She smiled again. 'Why don't you guys go and get the fire going.' The pit was a far enough away from the main house that guests could enjoy hours sitting around without worrying they'd disturb her up at the house. 'Who would like another tea or coffee?'

While Georgie took drink orders, Annabel and Jed loaded dishes into the dishwasher and tided up the kitchen.

With everyone else around the fire, Zara snuck into Finn's room to check on him. He'd been exhausted from his sleepover and day with Ben. After his bath, she'd struggled to keep him awake long enough to eat dinner and he'd been sound asleep when everyone had arrived. She'd taken the monitor outside and kept it with her in case he stirred, but he hadn't moved a muscle.

She was straightening his covers when she heard movement. She jumped and turned around. Ben was leaning against the doorframe.

'Sorry, Zars, I didn't mean to startle you.'

After making sure the camera was still on, she softly closed the door and led Ben back to the lounge room. It was clear he had something on his mind.

She sat on the edge of the couch and Ben sat beside her.

'You don't like him, do you?' she asked. Ben had been quiet tonight.

'It's not that. He seems like a great guy.'

'Then, what?'

Ben scrubbed his face with his hand. 'I've never seen you look at someone the way you look at him.'

'Is that a bad thing?'

'Not at all. It's just I want you to be careful. And think about Finn.'

'I haven't stopped thinking about him.' She inhaled and exhaled loudly. Ben loved her, and Finn, and he was within his rights to be concerned but his slightly judgmental tone was making her feel snitchy. 'I know you're concerned, Ben. I can read you like a book. All I can do is promise I won't go too fast. Ryan seems like a lovely guy, but nothing—no-one—will come between me and Finn. He's my number one man.'

'I thought I was your number one man,' Ben said with a wink.

With that, the tension eased, and Zara chuckled. 'So that's the problem. You're jealous.'

'Not jealous. Just being cautious. Do you know much about him?'

'Probably as much as you do. I take it you did your Google research before you came here tonight.'

Ben sighed. 'I did. And even though there was all that mess in Queensland a couple of months ago, it sounds like he didn't do anything wrong.'

'He didn't. It was his ex-girlfriend.'

'You're not concerned he's on the rebound? According to what I read; they only broke up two months ago.'

'No, I'm not concerned about that.'

Ben looked down at his feet before looking up and meeting her gaze. 'Will you tell him about me? About us?'

She hesitated. 'No. You and I promised each other Finn's paternity would remain our secret.'

'I don't think you should start a relationship with something that big between the two of you.'

Zara stiffened. She didn't remember asking Ben for his relationship advice.

Ben reached out and took her hand. 'Zara come on. We've been friends forever. It's not like this is the first time we've been this blunt with each other. Take my advice. If things get serious with you and this guy, I want you to tell him about him about me and Finn. I need you to.'

She chewed her bottom lip.

'You like him a lot, don't you?' Ben asked.

She pictured Ryan's face and the way he'd looked at her all night, his eyes full of admiration. 'I've never felt like this with anyone,' she replied softly. 'Ever.'

'Then tell him, Zara,' Ben said, equally as quiet. 'If you trust him, I trust you and your judgment.'

'Thanks, Ben.' She squeezed his hand then let it go. 'You know how much I love you, right?'

'And I love you too, Zazu. Even though you sometimes drive me up the wall.'

She chuckled. 'Isn't that what friends are for?'

They headed back outside. When Annabel spotted them, she headed over, slipping her hand into Ben's. 'I think we might head off if that's okay.'

Ben smiled at his wife, then Zara. 'Yeah, good idea. It's getting late. Thanks for inviting us, Zars. It was a great night.'

Jed and Georgie joined them.

'We're going to get going too,' Jed said.

'Yeah, sorry, Zars, I'm wiped, and I have an early start,' Georgie added, giving Zara a hug.

'Do you need a hand with anything before we go?' Ben asked.

'All sorted,' Ryan said, coming out of the dark to stand beside Zara.

He draped an arm over her shoulder and even though Zara sensed Ben watching, she ignored him.

'I'll make sure everything's tidy before we head off tonight,' Ben added.

'Thanks for coming, guys,' Zara said, acutely aware of the weight and warmth of Ryan's arm.

Jed extended his hand towards Ryan. 'It was great to meet you, mate.'

'It was good to meet you, too.'

'Will I see you next week at training?' Jed asked.

'You're persistent,' Ryan replied with a smile. 'I'll see.'

'I call it stubborn,' Georgie replied. 'Honestly Ryan, if you're too busy getting settled into the clinic, just say no.'

'I'll see how I go.'

With a wave, Ben and Annabel headed to their car. Jed and Ryan walked ahead of Zara and Georgie, talking about football.

Georgie leaned in towards Zara. 'He's a keeper. A real sweetie. I'm not imagining the sparks flying between you two, am I?'

Unable to pull her gaze away from Ryan who was deep in discussion with Jed, Zara shook her head. 'You're not imagining it.'

Georgie hooked her arm through Zara's. 'Will you sleep with him?'

'Not yet. It's too soon. I want to get to know him better and I want to see how he is with Finn. No point getting my heart broken because I've fallen in love with him if Finn doesn't like him.'

'That's wise.'

Ryan glanced their way and when his gaze locked on Zara's her breath caught and her heart did a little flip.

Georgie smiled. 'I love the way he looks at you like that. The guy is smitten.'

'But surely it's too quick.' From the moment Ryan had first kissed her, he'd thrown her world off-kilter. Perhaps she should put the brakes on.

'It was the same for me and Jed,' Georgie said. 'No matter how much I tried to fight it, I knew we were meant to be together.'

'But it's only been three days. Am I rushing things?'

'Not necessarily. You *could* take things slowly, but why? Maybe this is love at first sight.'

Zara grimaced. 'You and your romantic rubbish. You read too many books. I thought you were the logical sensible one in our friendship.'

'And I thought you were the risk taker,' Georgie countered.

'Not anymore. Not now I have Finn.'

'Of course. And fair enough. But seriously, Zars, I've watched the two of you together all night. I think he might be good for you.'

A lump formed in the back of Zara's throat. 'I just don't want Finn to get hurt.'

'If Ryan's the right person for you, he'll love Finn. Just give them time to get to know each other.'

'In other words, go slow.'

'Not necessarily. Just make sure Finn's included in things and give them both a chance to get to know each other. You never know, Ryan might make a great dad.'

Zara's stomach clenched. Georgie didn't have to say what she was thinking because Zara had already thought it. Finn needed a father figure and Ryan could be that person.

Jed called out for Georgie to go and she gave Zara another quick hug. 'Just give him a chance,' she said before walking to the car.

After her friends had driven off, Ryan came and stood with her, sliding his arm around her waist and pulling her close to his side. 'I hope you're going to join me by the fire,' he said softly.

She looked up at him and his smile made her heart flutter. He was so close it would have been easy for her to reach up on her toes and kiss him. He caressed her cheek with the back of his hand and her skin tingled at the touch. It took all her willpower to step back.

'You probably should get back to the fire and your friends. This is your last chance to spend time with them before the wedding next weekend.'

'I'd rather spend the rest of the night with you.'

She slid her gaze back to his and in the dim light saw the desire in his eyes.

'I don't want this day to end, Zara. At least not without you by my side.'

'I feel the same,' she murmured.

'Then come and join us around the fire.'

'As long as I'm not in the way.'

'You won't be.'

'Okay.' She smiled up at him. 'Let me just head inside and check on Finn again and grab a heavier jacket.'

*

Finn was still sound asleep. She leaned down and kissed the top of his head, then straightened the covers. Her mind was all over the place. She could just imagine the conversation Jed and Georgie were having on the way home.

Ryan hadn't hidden his feelings for her. During dinner, he'd sat next to her, touching her arm or shoulder often. The crazy thing was, no-one seemed to think it was odd. It was as if the entire group had concluded that it was perfectly normal for two people to get together so quickly. Even Ryan's mates acted like it was no big deal.

The only one who'd been quiet was Ben and she now knew why. She sighed softly. Ben was right. If she was going to start anything serious with Ryan, he needed to know about Ben and Finn up front. But would telling him make him run?

Zara opened the blind on Finn's bedroom window and looked out. She could just make out the yellow and orange fire licking up from the fire pit. There was nothing more relaxing than sitting around the fire toasting marshmallows and watching the stars. But as much as she itched to be out there with Ryan, she didn't really want to be there with him and his friends. She wanted him alone.

After grabbing her coat, she checked her reflection in the bathroom mirror, quickly brushing her hair and applying some lip gloss before heading outside.

The smell of the fire mingled with the men's voices and tension tightened her shoulders. As she walked down the hill from the house, she forced herself to relax. If she got to the fire and it was clear the men wanted to be left alone, she'd say her goodnights and head back to the house. There was plenty of time to catch up with Ryan alone tomorrow.

'I was wondering what was taking you so long.' Ryan's voice sounded from the shadows.

He was sitting on a log on the other side of the fire, a stick in his hand, toasting a marshmallow. When their eyes locked, her heart gave an extra beat.

'We were just going to call it a night,' Hamish said, standing abruptly. 'Right, guys?'

Dan and Rob looked from Hamish to Ryan to Zara. 'Yeah, that's right,' Rob said, also standing. 'Early start tomorrow.'

'Yep, it's time we hit the hay,' Dan agreed, stretching his arms and faking a yawn. 'Lucky for some.' He looked over at Ryan. 'You can sleep in tomorrow. We need to be gone early so we can get to the airport to catch our flight.'

'I might just bunk down on the couch again at your place,' Dan said to Hamish. 'That way Ryan won't wake me when he comes in later and I won't wake him tomorrow when we leave.'

'You don't have to do that,' Ryan protested.

Dan winked. 'Reckon you might like to have the cottage to yourself tonight.'

'It's been a great weekend,' Hamish said. 'Thanks, Zara. Your place is terrific. Just confirming we will leave the keys in the lock box outside the cottage.'

'Yep, that's right. Thanks, guys. All the best for your wedding, Hamish.'

The men disappeared into the dark towards the cottages, leaving Zara and Ryan standing beside the fire in silence.

'Want a marshmallow?' Ryan asked, holding up the charred remains of the one on the end of his twig.

'I'll pass.'

'Can you hear Finn from here?' Ryan asked.

She touched the pocket of her jacket. 'I have a monitor here. If he wakes up, I'll hear him, and I can run back to the house. It's not far.'

He patted the log he was sitting on. 'Come and sit next to me. The smoke is blowing the other way.'

They sat in silence for a while. Zara watched as he carefully pierced two marshmallows with the end of the stick and put them near the coals.

'Your friend, Ben, was watching me like a hawk tonight.'

'Yeah, sorry about that.'

'Doesn't bother me. Like I said, it's clear there's a lot of history between the two of you.'

'A lot.'

He grinned. 'What did you tell him about us?' He pulled the marshmallows from the fire and blew on them to cool them down before offering one to her.

'I told him I want to take things slowly.'

'Do you?' he murmured.

'No.'

'Neither do I.' He tossed the stick into the fire and pulled her closer to him, turning slightly to face her. 'I've never wanted another woman the way I want you. I like you a lot. It's not just the chemistry between us, Zara, I admire you and really want to get to know you better.

She exhaled in a rush. 'I like you, too.'

He raised his eyebrows but said nothing.

She groaned, then bit her bottom lip. 'Maybe we *should* go slow.'

'We could. Or perhaps we could do this instead.'

He tugged her closer and wrapped his arms around her waist before kissing her hard on the lips.

Chapter Nineteen

Zara's squeak of surprise was cut off by Ryan's lips against hers. She told herself to pull away, but the rational side of her brain lost out. She could no more stop what they were doing, than she could've stopped a train. And that was what this was. A runaway train of desire for Ryan Dunlop. There was nothing she could do or wanted to do but hold on and enjoy the ride.

He deepened the kiss and she moaned as she wound her arms around his neck. He tasted her and gently demanded her response, which she willingly gave. She loved that Ryan didn't treat her with kid gloves but kissed her with passion and desire that was almost fierce in its tenderness.

'Oh, Ryan.'

His mouth slid from hers and he began to dot kisses down her jawline. Her head was spinning. His lips claimed hers again and it was hard to think straight.

'I want you so much,' he murmured against her throat.

His husky admission sent heat gathering low in her belly and her insides twisted with desire.

'I want you too, Ryan.'

He pulled back and blinked and Zara saw satisfaction register in his eyes. When he kissed her again, her knees buckled, and she might have hit the ground if he hadn't caught her around the waist and pulled her closer.

'You are so beautiful, Zara.' He gently slipped a hand between them and moved it up her rib cage to gently cup the underside of her breast. 'Is this alright?'

She nodded. 'But not here.'

A low, growl rose from his throat. 'Thank God the guys are all staying together in the one cottage. Mine is empty if you're keen.'

'Very keen.'

'Let's cover this fire first and make sure it's safe.'

It didn't take them long to spread some dirt over the logs and douse the flames in water. He caught her hand and pulled her towards his cottage, his brisk stride turning into a run. Zara laughed with joy, keeping up with ease.

By the time they reached Ryan's cottage, she was trembling with a mix of need and apprehension. He ushered her inside first, then closed the door behind them, leaning against it to catch his breath. After a few seconds he pushed away from the door and walked over to switch on a lamp. In the soft glow, his gaze was hot with passion. Zara's heart thundered and an ache grew inside her.

'Are you nervous?' He asked, slowly walking towards her.

She nodded. There was no point in lying. 'Absolutely. It's been a long time.' Years since she'd been intimate with anyone—male or female. So long ago she wasn't sure she'd remember what to do.

'I'm nervous too.'

Ryan's honest admission surprised her. What did he have to be nervous about?

After easing off her jacket, he tugged her jumper and t-shirt up and over her head. She resisted the urge to cover up her breasts. The plastic surgeon had done a remarkable job and they were a testament to her survival, but she was still self-conscious of them.

'You are so beautiful,' he murmured. 'I want to see you. All of you.'

His teasing touch sent shivers through her as if she was being zapped by one of the electric fences. As he pressed himself to her, her body buzzed with excitement. He caught the back of her neck, pulling her closer and his mouth covered hers again, his tongue pressing past her closed lips.

She pulled away. 'I want to see you, too,' she pleaded hoarsely.

With a groan he lifted his head from kissing her throat and let her unbutton his shirt and tug at his clothes.

Her mouth went dry and a wave of hot and cold went through her.

'Come here, Zara.'

He didn't need to ask twice.

*

Afterwards, Zara tucked closer to Ryan in his warm and cosy bed. Warmth stole through every inch of her, but especially her heart. With Ryan's arms around her and his lips brushing her forehead, she could have stayed here for eternity. She snuggled closer. His arms tightened and his chest rose against her cheek as he breathed deeply.

She slow-blinked, drowsiness slipping over her like early morning fog. A sound from the couch made her jerk in his arms and gasp.

Ryan froze. 'What was that?'

She gasped and sat up, pulling the sheet to cover her nakedness. 'The monitor. Finn.'

Ryan swore.

Her heart twisted, her breath lodged in her throat and she felt sick. What sort of mother was she that she'd left her child effectively on his own so she could have sex?

She hastily pulled on her knickers, then her jeans. 'I'm sorry, Ryan.'

He swung his legs out of bed. 'You don't need to apologise. I do. I should have thought of Finn first.'

Another rustling sound came from the monitor.

'You'd better go.'

She was already out the door and sprinting up the track from the cottage to her house, berating herself with every breath.

When she pushed open the back door, she expected to see Finn blearily looking for her, but he was still in his own bed, sound asleep. She exhaled heavily. How could she have left him alone? If anyone found out, they'd call the social services. This couldn't happen again.

Zara caught a glimpse of herself in the hallway mirror. Her cheeks were flushed, and her eyes shone. A wave of heat washed over her as she recalled the way Ryan had touched her. Followed by an even bigger wave, this time of guilt. she'd left Finn alone. If she and Ryan were intimate again, it had to be at her place, not his, or when Finn was having a sleepover with her parents.

She needed to slow things down. For Finn's sake.

Chapter Twenty

The next few weeks were a blur. Ryan started his new job and couldn't believe how busy the clinic was. He'd been surprised how many people had come for their annual "check-ups" until he figured that was their way of checking *him* out. Although he still couldn't put a face to all their names, they all knew who he was. He was greeted by everyone with a cheery "Hey, Doc" or "Morning Doctor D". At first the familiarity from his patients had surprised him, but now he was used to it. Not surprisingly, no-one other than Zara called him Dr Delicious although she still did it now and then to tease him.

He was also getting used to being stopped in the street by a patient who wanted to have a chat about their current ailment. His stock standard line was "give the clinic a call and book in to see me."

Each night he headed back out to Braxton Park and had dinner with Zara and Finn. Even though there was a kitchen in the cottage he was renting, he often didn't have the energy to cook. He worried he was taking advantage of Zara's hospitality, but she was a far better cook than he was, and continually told him she loved the adult company. Some nights they ate with Finn, other nights the little boy had already eaten by the time Ryan got to her place. On those nights, he and Zara would eat together, often with a candle flickering on the table between them. Other times, by the time he got home, Zara would be already watching her favourite TV show. She'd point to the microwave with a grin, and he'd eat in silence until she let him talk during the ad breaks.

After three weeks, he'd stopped going back to his own cottage at night. Zara welcomed him into her bed and although he'd protested—admittedly very feebly at first, worried about what Finn would think—she'd assured him it was more than okay.

They'd slipped into an easy routine during the week and, on weekends when Zara's mum or Ben and Annabel looked after Finn, they went riding.

In the midst of all that, guests came and went from the cottages. And Andy showed up every Saturday morning, as arranged, to help Zara with the horses.

It didn't take long for Ryan to consider Zara his friend and his confidante, not just his lover. He'd quickly discovered she was someone he could talk to and someone he could trust. In between caring for Finn or helping her with the horses or doing odd jobs together on the farm, he found himself talking to her about all kinds of things. He'd even joked she was cheaper and better than any counsellor he'd ever had. He still hadn't told her about Lisa and the baby, but he would, when the time was right.

The best part was getting to know Finn. Zara had told him Finn was usually reserved around people he didn't know, but from day one, he'd seemed to like Ryan. Some days Ryan wondered if, somewhere deep in his soul, Finn knew Ryan had been there at his birth.

*

On the middle weekend in September, Ryan was in town waiting for the bakery to open. It was grand final day and Glengarrick were favourites to win the premiership cup—again. A handful of regulars stood with him and although he didn't remember all their names, over the past six weeks he'd met them all either through the clinic or when he came into town. The talk was all about the match.

Ryan was feeling positive about the game, but a nervous energy coursed through him. Twice a week for the past six weeks he'd been at training and was now invested in the team. At first the boys had been polite, but understandably wary after the burpees incident, but when they realised who he was and what professional expertise he brought with him, they warmed up.

Even though he didn't need to be at the ground until ten o'clock, he liked to get there well before the players and help Jed out. In a few short weeks, Jed had become a good mate and Ryan looked forward to spending more time with him and Georgie after the season was over.

After grabbing his coffee, he stopped at the newsagent to pick up the local paper along with the Melbourne papers he liked to read. The headline from the local rag caught his eye and he smiled again. "'Best talent in years', says Glengarrick's new doctor." He chuckled. He had no memory of anyone asking him to make a comment for the paper.

'What's up, Doc?'

Ryan turned and saw old Arthur Wheaton walking towards him. The man was ninety-three and fit as a Mallee bull, as he liked to constantly remind everyone.

'Bloody cold, eh?' Arthur pulled his jacket more tightly around him. 'You go for a ride this morning?'

Ryan chuckled. 'Not this morning. I've got a big day at the oval.'

As soon as Arthur had found out Ryan loved to ride, the old man took every opportunity to tell Ryan he'd been a champion horseman "back in his day". Ryan did some digging and discovered Arthur wasn't lying. He should have made the Australian Olympic team, but he'd broken a leg chasing sheep on his horse on the family farm and had to give up his Olympic dreams.

Arthur pointed to the newspaper in Ryan's hands. 'Reckon Jed's feeling the pressure?'

'No. Stuff like this doesn't get to him. Not after winning three premierships for Geelong.'

'Guess you're used to pressure too.'

'Yeah.'

When Ryan had first come to town, he'd figured it would be a good place to hide his past. He was wrong. Everyone knew about the accusations and how he'd lost his job. Whether they believed his innocence or not, time would tell, but so far, he didn't get any sense they were holding it against him. If anything, his notoriety had probably helped him pick up new patients—many of whom hadn't been to a GP for years and other who used to travel to larger towns to get medical treatment.

He and Arthur chatted for a while about the game with Arthur discussing every individual player's strengths and weaknesses. Ryan was about to tell Arthur he should ask Jed for a job as assistant coach when Arthur sucked in a quick breath and leaned in.

'Look out. Here's trouble.'

Ryan turned to see Tubby Stevens heading towards them.

'G'day, Arthur. Doc.' He nodded at Ryan. 'What's goin' on?'

'Nothing much,' Arthur said. 'Just chatting to Doc Ryan here about the weather.'

With perfect timing, to emphasise the lie, a dirty farm ute drove by making them all step back to avoid being splashed by mud.

'Heard Glengarrick doesn't have a chance,' Tubby said.

'Is that right?' Ryan asked.

'About time another team knocked bloody Glengarrick off their pedestal.'

'Maybe. I heard Derrinallum have been playing very well. I guess we'll see, won't we?'

Tubby cast a sideways look at Arthur, then Ryan. 'Either of you wanna put a bet on it?'

Arthur shook his head.

Ryan had heard there was a small group of men who ran a betting book on local games, making up their own odds. Tubby started to bite his nails, and after a second of silence, he leaned in and said, 'What do ya reckon, Doc? Fancy a bet on the game?'

A battered old station wagon pulled up next to them. 'Hey, Arthur. Want a lift to the ground?'

It was Bruce, another one of Ryan's patients.

'Nah, she's right,' Arthur said. 'I've got a few things to do before I head over there.'

Bruce waved and drove off, a blue-grey cloud following his car.

'What about it, Doc?'

Tubby didn't give up easily.

'No, sorry. I don't bet on football. In fact, I don't bet on anything.' Ryan's uncle had been a gambler, and he'd lost everything, including his family. It was a lesson Ryan had learned early and it had made a huge impact on him.

'Right.'

'But I can give you some inside information, if that will help,' Ryan said.

Tubby shuffled on the spot and rubbed his hands together. 'I knew I'd come to the right man.'

Arthur frowned at Ryan.

'You want to know what our game plan is?' Ryan rested his hand on Tubby's bony shoulder. The man looked up at Ryan like a puppy about to get a leg of lamb he knew would be too big to carry.

Ryan glanced around as though to he didn't want anyone to overhear, then leaned in and lowered his voice. 'Glengarrick's game plan is simple. We're going to *win*.'

Tubby's eyes narrowed. 'Very bloody funny. That's hardly inside information. I reckoned out of anyone, you'd be happy to sell out on your team. Heard that's what happened up in Queensland.'

Ryan glared at him. 'You heard wrong.'

Without another word, Ryan turned and walked away.

Chapter Twenty-One

Ryan was still annoyed by the time he arrived at the ground. Arthur had wisely given him space to walk alone, Ryan's long strides taking almost half the time it usually took him to walk from the main street to the football oval. Was he ever going to be able to move on from what had happened in Queensland or was the cloud of suspicion going to follow him to his grave?

By the time he turned in at the gates, the light rain had eased, and he slowed his steps. The last thing Jed or the players needed was for him to be in a foul mood. As he headed for the change rooms to see if anyone else had arrived, he took in the atmosphere. The women's teams were on the ground and there were hundreds of supporters lining the oval cheering them on.

On the nearby netball courts, there were games in progress and wherever he looked, Glengarrick Saints club beanies were being proudly worn. A group of primary school aged kids played kick-to-kick near the playground, and the footy mums were busy at the canteen. He spotted at least a half dozen homemade banners at one end of the ground. In the middle of the small group of people was Pat Lockhead, the local librarian, who, ironically, was one of the loudest and most vocal of the supporters.

At the other end of the ground was Pat's husband, Bill. He was a huge man—a heart attack waiting to happen—but everyone said he had the best eye and was one of the top umpires in the league. His other claim to fame was regularly winning the pie-eating contest at the annual Football Fundraiser. These days, because he found it too hard to run with the other umpires up and down the ground, he was happy to wave his flags with great enthusiasm with every score.

A handful of players had already arrived and were doing warm up sprints under Jed's direction. On the other side of the oval, away from the crowd, the other team—the Derrinallum Dragons— were doing their own warm up routine.

A light breeze had blown the drizzle away and the sun was surprisingly warm. At least no one could complain about a wind advantage for either side.

Jed came over after a few minutes and shook Ryan's hand and slapped him on the back.

'There's not a spare car park within cooee.' Ryan said. 'Looks like the whole town's turned up.'

'They usually do,' Jed replied.

They parted and Jed headed off to gather his players together for one last huddle before the game started. Ryan went to his position on the boundary and introduced himself to the physio and myotherapist who were busy strapping shoulders and ankles. He left them to it—he'd only be needed if there was an injury they were concerned about.

*

By the last quarter, it wasn't clear whether Glengarrick had what it took to win. Derrinallum were fighting hard, and the Glengarrick players were struggling even after the three-quarter time pep talk Jed had given them.

After a heavy bump, one of the Glengarrick players picked himself up from the ground. A tiny trickle of blood seeped down his cheek from his temple and Ryan called him over. As he quickly applied a dressing and sent the player back out again, he heard the thump of the ball as one of the Derrinallum players booted it out of defence. The umpire jogged back to the point where the ball had crossed the boundary line for the throw-in.

Moments later Derrinallum had the ball, but their player's kick was messy off the left boot. Bent over, hands on his knees, he gasped for air. He'd narrowly missed what could have been the goal to win the game. Ryan couldn't muster any sympathy for the player's disappointment. He was too relieved that Glengarrick was still in the game.

Back in the centre, the two ruckmen were like gladiators, locked in battle for position, each one pushing against the other for territory. The umpire arched his back, heaving the ball over his head before bouncing it into play. The bodies of the two rucks flew into the air and the crowd noise fell as the ball curved in the breeze, the trajectory favouring Derrinallum. Archer thrust his bulk sideways with a grunt that could be heard across the ground and nudged his opponent, but it wasn't enough, and the Derrinallum player tapped it out as the ball was making its descent. The ball went straight into the chest of the Saints' James Malloy, and the crowd's roar quickly turned into a shout as two players locked him in bruising tackles.

Ryan glanced up and saw Zara and Finn heading his way. He gave them a wave before turning his attention back to the game. They came and stood near him, close enough he felt their presence, but not so close as to stop him from concentrating on the game. Still, it was a struggle to keep his eye on the game and not on Zara.

A player—a giant of a man from Derrinallum—was thundering towards the boundary, desperate to make it to the contest in time. Mud flew from his boots and smaller players parted to clear the way. With fatigue slowing his pace, Tom Wilson, one of the Glengarrick player tried to stop him but the Derrinallum player slammed his shoulder into Tom who was a good ten centimetres shorter. He fell to the ground, pain twisting his face.

Ryan was running onto the field, headed straight for Tom before Jed had even shouted for him.

'You okay?' Ryan asked.

'Winded.'

'Want to come off?'

Tom shook his head, staggered to his feet and jogged back into position.

Ryan shrugged as he walked back to Zara. 'I swear some of these guys are tougher than the AFL players.'

From the corner of his eye, he caught a glimpse of Tom, exploding from halfback, screaming for the ball. The tackle spun Archer around in mid-air and he fell to the ground. Arms still free, he somehow managed to lob a handpass high over his head and the crowd roared as Tom caught it then stepped right, dodging a lunging defender. He accelerated again as his teammates yelled 'You're clear! Clear!' and bounced the ball. One stride, then another, then another then he bounced it again. Ryan watched in awe. If Tom played like this for the selectors, he'd be first pick. No one could catch him.

All around the ground on the sidelines, spectators cupped their hands around their mouths and yelled for all they were worth.

'Go, son!'

'Go, you bloody good thing.'

'Tommo!'

Richie Clark set off towards centre half-forward like a racehorse as Tom dashed up the wing towards him. He spotted

Richie and took one more step to steady, then leant back and guided the ball gently to his boot. His right foot stabbed it low and sharp, like a missile and it landed with a loud thwack straight into Richie's outstretched hands.

The shrill of the umpire's whistle sounded the mark but the thunderous boom from the crowd drowned it out. The ball was in the hands of their leading goal kicker directly in front of the posts. This was it, the kick that would put Glengarrick in the lead with only seconds to go.

There was a hush as Richie walked back to his mark, ball on his hip. A hush fell over the ground as Richie went through his customary preparation: resting the ball on the ground like it was a fragile egg, pulling up each of his blue and white striped socks.

The Derrinallum defender was yelling and punching the air, star jumping. Doing anything he could to try to distract Richie. If he missed this, Glengarrick would lose the grand final.

Amidst frenzied booing from the Derrinallum cheer squad and some of the crowd, Richie cantered towards goal. He took his usual ten steps, then leaned back and calmly booted a fifty-metre drop punt.

The goal umpire shuffled towards the left-hand goalpost, crouched, watching it soar over his head as the crowd held their breath. Then, standing tall, feet together, eyes forward with the deadpan face common to all goal umpires, the man in white raised both hands, forefingers pointing, signifying the goal. The crowd went wild, and a deafening cheer rose from around the ground.

With only seconds, maybe a minute left, Ryan sent up a prayer that the final siren would come. He swung his eyes from the scoreboard to the players and saw the tiredness of men who had spent every bit of energy they possessed, half of them with hands on their knees, bent over, gasping for air.

As the field umpire jogged the ball back to the middle for what would be the final centre bounce, a loud blast sounded like a trumpet across the ground. Time seemed to slow as the realisation set in. Glengarrick had won again.

Jed slapped Ryan on the back as he leapt over the boundary fence and joined the blue-and-white clad Saint's supporters who had flooded the ground. Ryan followed him, avoiding the Derrinallum players lying exhausted in the mud. Strangers hugged strangers and people crowded around the players, laughing and shaking hands, high fiving and thumping backs.

Ryan grinned. He loved this grass roots version of the game.

Chapter Twenty-Two

Ryan was spending his Sunday morning working the horses with Zara. Finn was with Zara's mum for the day. Ryan watched as she cantered Colby in the newly set up aluminium round yard in the large paddock next to the stables. Her hold on the reins was confident and relaxed. Zara was a natural in the saddle and she and her horse looked good together. So good in fact, it was hard to keep his mind on his own job.

Melody was one of the new horses that had come from a racehorse trainer, and she was his charge for the moment. For now, he was taking it easy on her, just walking her around the open paddock and letting her relax in her new surroundings.

He smiled again at Zara. His admiration of her had further escalated. Ever since she'd taken up the idea of running an equine therapy program at Braxton Park, she'd been a woman on a mission. At night, after Finn was in bed, she spent hours online, researching. The way she was going, it would only be a matter of months before she had the new business up and running.

She'd already spoken to a number of horse trainers who were willing to give her retired racehorses to rehabilitate and use as therapy horses including Melody, the horse he was currently walking around.

Zara glanced over at him, grinned and waved. He waved back. The early morning sun hit Colby's gleaming chestnut coat and reflected off the bling on Zara's new helmet he'd bought her as a gift.

He was on the other side of the paddock, about a hundred meters from Zara, walking Melody on a loose rein when movement out of the corner of his eye caught his attention. When he turned, every muscle in his body tensed and his stomach went into free fall. The next-door neighbour's black bull was barrelling wildly towards Zara and Colby in the round yard. Neither of them had seen it.

The warning cry that escaped Ryan's throat was futile. He was too far away and there was no way Zara could hear him, but he couldn't stop the shout, any more than he could stop the danger heading directly towards her. The lightweight fencing would be no barrier to a charging bull. Knowing it was foolhardy, he spun Melody into action, and the mare took off, flat out, as if she were racing in the Melbourne Cup.

The wind rushing past his ears didn't mask the deadening thud as the bull charged headfirst into the round yard metal fencing. He pictured Colby and the bull in a head-on collision, flesh on flesh and knew the force of six hundred kilograms from each direction could kill either animal, or Zara.

He heard a scream and he drove Melody on with his hands and voice, pushing her for more speed. The bull hit the fence again, knocking one section over. Zara flew off Colby's back, landing with a thud. The bull thundered after Colby as Ryan's horse bucked and weaved to avoid it. Colby was too fast for the bull and it either tired of its game or changed its mind, crashing through a wire fence and disappearing into a neighbouring property.

The distance between himself and Zara seemed endless, like a nightmare where he'd never reach the disaster waiting just in front of him. Metres from the broken fencing, he sat back in the saddle and Melody's hocks dropped, her hind feet leaving a trail in the slippery grass with a halt that would have made a rodeo horse proud.

Ryan was out of the saddle and running towards Zara in a single motion, leaving Melody to stand. He heard thundering hooves and turned to see Colby running along the fence line, nostrils flaring, ribcage heaving.

Ryan dropped to his knees beside Zara. Forcing aside his panic at her unconscious form, he gripped his professionalism with both hands. He wanted to take off her helmet and straighten her body and make her unconscious crumpled more comfortable, but it was the worst thing to do. Reaching out, he touched her face lightly with the back of his hand. Her cheek was cool and clammy, shock already taking over with uncompromising relentlessness.

He pulled his phone from his pocket and dialled 000. While he waited to be connected, he stilled his fingers and his own racing heart long enough to find her pulse. It was rapid but weak, just below her jawline. He couldn't see any obvious blood, but by the angle of her leg, it was definitely broken.

'Police, fire or ambulance.'

'Ambulance.'

'Which state and town are you calling from?'

'Victoria. Glengarrick. Near Stockton,' he replied breathlessly.

'Please hold the line while I connect you.'

Once he'd explained to the operator what had happened, he sat back to wait. There was nothing he could do except monitor Zara's shallow breathing and pray. Even if he'd had his doctor's bag with him, there was nothing in it that would help Zara.

The ambulance must have been in the area, because it came down the drive about ten minutes later. Though those ten minutes felt more like an hour.

Ryan answered the paramedic's questions and gave his medical opinion while the paramedics worked, but as much as he wanted to help, he couldn't do anything until Zara had her neck immobilised and she was on a stretcher.

He assisted the paramedics by holding Zara's head while they strapped the plastic collar to her and gently straightened her body.

At worst she'd broken her back. At best, it was just the fractured femur.

He heard a car and glanced up. A man ran over.

'I heard the ambulance. Is everything okay?'

'Zara's had a fall. Her horse got spooked by a bull.'

The man swore. 'That bloody bull. I told Dad he needed to fix the fencing.' He scrubbed his beard. 'I'm Matt. Zara's neighbour. Can I give you a hand with the horses?'

Ryan looked over to where Melody and Colby stood, reins dragging on the ground. 'I need to stay with Zara. Can you take the horses into the shed and take off their tack?'

'Yeah, sure can.'

For the next few minutes as they loaded Zara into the back of the ambulance, Ryan felt like he was the only one not doing anything. Once the ambulance had departed, lights flashing but silent, he walked over to shed, feeling like he was moving through deep sludge. He wanted to follow the ambulance, but Zara would want him to make sure the horses were okay. He didn't want to put them back in the paddock until he knew they were settled.

Back in the shed, he and Matt checked the horses together. Colby's breath blew warm on Ryan's arm, and he placed a hand at the origin of the long white marking on his face before running his hands over her body and down each leg. Surprisingly, Colby didn't seem to be hurt.

As soon as he'd finished with the horses he headed to the hospital in Stockton. Parking his car out the front, he followed the signs to the entrance and hurried inside, only to be directed to a waiting room. He perched on the edge of a plastic chair, alone amid the other people waiting for treatment. Pulling out his phone, he texted Ben to ask if he could look after Finn a bit longer. He didn't want to call anyone else when he had no news to offer them.

About half an hour later a woman in navy scrubs appeared. She scanned the room and when she caught Ryan's gaze, she offered him a small smile which told him nothing. He stood, straightened his shoulders and reached out his hand.

'Ryan Dunlop.'

'Hi I'm Natalie. One of the doctors. Are you Zara's next of kin?'

'Ah, no.'

'Oh.' She frowned.

'I'm her partner. And I'm a doctor too. I'm the GP in Glengarrick,' he added quickly.

Natalie smiled. 'Nice to meet you. You're filling in for Laura. I hear you're doing a great job and the locals love you.'

'Thanks. Listen, I was with Zara when the accident happened. I haven't called any of her family yet because I didn't know what to tell them. I thought I'd wait until after she'd had x-rays.'

'Of course. Well, come on through.'

Ryan followed Natalie through a door to the emergency department.

'Your girlfriend is incredibly lucky,' Natalie said, over her shoulder.

'Is she conscious?'

'Yes.'

'What about…' He hesitated, almost too scared to ask.

Natalie kept talking as she strode down the corridor past cubicles and pushed open another door that led to a ward. 'She's stable. We've done imaging and there are no internal injuries.'

'Head trauma? Spinal?'

'She's broken a rib, but her lungs are okay. The worst of it is a fractured left femur. She's broken it in three places.'

He exhaled in a rush. It was a miracle she'd gotten off that easily. He'd feared it was so much worse, when she'd been lying there in the sand in the middle of the round yard. People died in wrecks like that.

'Will she need surgery?'

Natalie nodded. 'Definitely. But she'll have to go to Melbourne for that. We'll stabilise her here on the ward tonight and keep the pain relief up to her and she'll be transferred in the morning.'

Natalie pushed a door open and held it, waiting for him to go through.

'I'll leave you to it. Nice to meet you, Ryan. I'm sure we'll bump into each other again.'

'Thanks, Natalie.'

Ryan closed the door softly behind him, not wanting to disturb Zara if she was sleeping. She was alone in a two-bed hospital room on the side closest to the window. He stood rooted at the door, silently watching her. Her eyes were closed, and her face was ashen with dark smudges under her eyes from where her makeup had run. Fluids hung from the IV pole and dripped into the cannula in her left hand.

She must have sensed someone there, because she turned her head and opened her eyes. She attempted a smile, but it was more of a grimace. He walked to the edge of the bed and took her free hand.

'Hey.'

'Ryan,' she said softly. 'What happened?'

He chose his words carefully. He didn't want to alarm her too much. 'Colby got spooked and he threw you.'

Eyebrows lifted then a crease in her brow formed, deepening as worry built on top of pain. 'Colby?'

'He's fine. Uninjured. When I left your place, he was happily munching on a biscuit of hay.'

She closed her eyes and exhaled slowly.

He pulled up a chair next to the bed and sat, stroking the back of her hand gently.

'Just so you know, they weren't going to let me in, so I had to tell them we're married.'

Her eyes snapped open.

'Just joking.'

She tried to laugh but it quickly turned into a scowl. 'Don't make me laugh, please.'

'Oh, crap. Sorry. The doctor said you've broken a few ribs.'

'Yeah. But I'll be okay.'

Her smile sent a surge of relief through him. He couldn't believe how strong she was. She had to be in agony, yet she was still offering him reassurance.

Her eyes closed again, as if the lids were too heavy and when she struggled to open them and look directly at him, his chest tightened.

'Will you stay with me?'

He leaned over and kissed her tenderly on the forehead. 'Of course, I will.'

As if he was going to leave.

*

Zara's stirring woke him around five a.m. He'd been dozing in the chair beside the bed.

He sat up, rubbed his eyes and looked over at her. 'Hey there. You're awake.'

She nodded. 'Did you stay here all night?' Her voice sounded scratchy, somewhere between a whisper and a croak.

He stood and leaned down to smooth her hair back from her forehead. 'I told you I wasn't going anywhere, remember?'

'You're going to need a chiropractor to fix your back,' she said. 'You looked like a pretzel in that chair.'

'Don't worry about me. How are you feeling?'

'Like crap. I have a monumental headache and my ribs are killing me. They hurt worse than my leg.'

'They put a nerve block in, remember? That's why you can't really feel your leg.'

She nodded, looking dazed. 'I feel like someone has pinned it to the bed.' She glanced behind him. 'What time is it?'

'About five.'

'I shouldn't have asked you to stay. You look exhausted.'

'I'll be fine. I can sleep when I get home. I'm taking the day off.'

She frowned. 'What about the clinic?'

'We can reschedule the patients. Anyone urgent can head into the hospital. Once news gets out that you're in hospital, they'll understand.' As soon as their relationship became public, the locals had taken him in like a prodigal son.

'I wish I could put into words how much it means to me that you stayed. Saying thank you seems wildly inadequate, but right now I'm too tired and in too much pain to find the right words.'

'Shall I buzz for the nurse?'

'Yes please.'

He pressed the buzzer, then took her hand. 'You're going to be okay.'

'I'm really scared about the surgery,' she said softly.

'You'll be okay. I'll be with you every step of the way and I'll help you with the horses while you recover.'

'Thank you.'

A few moments later the door opened, and a nurse entered. She handed Zara a paper glass of water and a small pill cup. 'I'll bet you're after some pain relief.'

Zara nodded. 'Thank you.' She swallowed the tablets and washed them down with the water.

'Are you hungry?' Ryan asked.

'Starving.'

The nurse grinned. 'Yeah, well sorry to break the bad news to you, but you have to fast. Your surgery is booked for this afternoon in Melbourne.'

'Your parents will be here soon too, to see you before you're transported to Melbourne.'

'And Finn?'

'They're bringing him too.'

Chapter Twenty-Three

On Friday, a week after surgery, Zara was getting used to navigating around the house on crutches. She was hoping that once her pain settled, she'd be able to hobble around a bit more without the crutches, even though the surgeons had told her she was to be fully non weight-bearing for eight weeks.

She put a bottle of water in a bag along with a book and headed for the back door. Catching up on her massive pile of books to be read was one good thing to come from breaking her leg.

Slinging the canvas bag over her shoulder, she reached for the handle on the back door, pushing it the rest of the way open with the end of a crutch, then eased outside onto the back veranda. The sun was shining and, although the breeze was cool, there were enough trees and shrubs to protect her from the wind.

She gently lowered herself into one of the outdoor timber chairs and lifted her cast-covered leg onto another chair. It took her a moment to sort out the pillows and get comfortable, but once she was, she sank back with a sigh. Until she got the cast off, recovery was going to be a slow road.

If it hadn't been for the countless visitors dropping by, she would have been lonely being on the farm without Finn and with Ryan at work every day. As it was, just as they had done when she was going through her cancer treatment, the locals had rallied to keep her in good spirits. She had help with showering, help with meals and cleaning and countless offers from people to help her with the horses or with Finn. Once again, she was blown away by everyone's care and concern.

But it was Ryan who shone. Both practically and emotionally he was there for her. There was no doubt in her mind that he was the kind of guy she could rely on.

Knowing how hard it would be for her to look after Finn and manage crutches, her parents had offered to take Finn for her, but after the first two days at home, she'd missed having him with her. When Ryan suggested he could drop Finn to her parents in the morning on his way to work and pick him up at the end of the day, it was the perfect solution for everyone.

The best thing about that was it gave Ryan and Finn time to build a relationship. Finn had already decided Ryan was his favourite person and had become his little shadow.

She smiled. How had she gotten so lucky? Ryan was steady, dependable and above all, compassionate. It had been easy to fall hard for him.

She was so engrossed in her book that she only realised it was starting to get dark when she heard his car pull up. She checked her watch, surprised it was after five o'clock but also curious as to why Ryan was home so early. He usually finished at five thirty, picked up Finn and got home around six.

'I'm out the back,' she called, although Ryan wouldn't be able to hear her. She heard his footsteps on the timber floors, then the back door opened.

She smiled but the little surge in her chest was temporary, fading rapidly, along with her smile, when she saw Ryan's face. The haggard and tired man standing in front of her looked markedly different from the happy man she'd last seen at breakfast. His hair was mussed and although his eyes matched the colour of his shirt, they weren't their usual vivid blue.

'Where's Finn?' she asked, frowning.

His shoulders sagged and he cursed under his breath. 'I'm sorry, he's still at your folks. It's been a crap day and I totally forgot about him. All I wanted to do was get home to you.'

A flicker of irritation went through her, but she pushed it aside. Ryan must have a very good reason to forget Finn. She reached for her phone. 'I'll call Mum. See if she's happy for him to stay overnight. I don't want her to drive out now. It's the worst time to be driving with the kangaroos.'

'I'm so sorry, Zara.'

'It's okay.' Right now, he looked like he'd crumble if she berated him.

While she called her mum, Ryan went back inside. She heard the shower running and when he came back out ten minutes later, he looked marginally better. He was carrying two glasses and a bottle of wine like some kind of peace offering.

'Let's start again.' He put the glasses down on the outdoor coffee table before leaning in and kissing her tenderly on the lips. 'Hey.'

'Hi,' she replied, tasting minty toothpaste on his breath.

She carefully shifted her cast off the seat opposite her and he sank into it with a sigh, running his hands through his hair and messing it further.

'Are you okay?' she asked carefully, because he still looked anything but alright.

'Not really.'

'Do you want to talk about it?'

'Can you give me a second?'

'Of course.'

Handing her both glasses, he poured a generous amount of wine into both of them. She handed one back to him and waited for him to clink glasses with her.

'To us,' she said.

He held her gaze and repeated the toast and it was the first time his smile had reached his eyes since he'd walked in. She allowed herself to relax a little. At least whatever was going on had nothing to do with their relationship.

After taking a sip of her wine, she sat back in the chair. He'd talk when he was ready.

After a couple of minutes that felt like an eternity, he still hadn't said a word. She usually didn't need to fill the gaps with words, but his silence was deafening.

'Mum and Dad were happy to have Finn overnight,' she said, realising she was sounding overly chatting and trying to compensate for the silence. 'Mum said she can bring him out tomorrow morning.'

'Or I can drive you in and we can pick him up. I can do the groceries while we're in town.'

'Only if it's not too much trouble. I wouldn't mind getting out of the house.'

He looked up and gently touched her cast. 'How's the leg feeling today?'

'Sore. But mostly just frustrating. Everything takes so much longer.' She smiled. 'But I have good nurses and a great doctor taking care of me, so I'll be fine.'

A crease formed between his brows and his lips pressed into a straight line. He glanced somewhere over her shoulder before his eyes fell back to her.

'What happened today, Ryan?' she asked gently.

'Is it okay if I don't talk about it now?' His words unfolded slowly, like he was having a tough time working them free. 'I just want to sit with you and forget about it for a bit.'

'Will you talk to me about it?'

He nodded. 'Just not right now.'

'Okay.'

He exhaled slowly. 'I'm sorry. That's not fair. I owe you an apology and an explanation. The thing is, I don't want to let you down and that's exactly what I've done.'

It was her turn to frown. What was he talking about? She shifted in the chair and leaned forward. 'You haven't let me down, Ryan. Ever. You go above and beyond, with everything. You've been amazing, especially since my accident.'

'Yet I forgot to pick Finn up tonight.'

'Whatever happened must have been serious for it to slip your mind. And you wouldn't be the first parent who has forgotten to pick up a child. No harm done. He's perfectly safe and happy with Mum and Dad and he knows no different.'

He ran his hands through his hair.

'It's okay. You didn't do it deliberately.'

'No, I didn't. I just had so much on my mind and all I could focus on was getting home to you and talking to you about it.'

'What happened?'

'One of my patients lost her baby today. Stillborn.'

'Oh, honey. That's awful.'

'It triggered a lot of memories for me.'

Zara waited.

'Remember I said I have lots of baggage?'

'And remember I said, so do I?' she asked, taking his hands in hers.

'I lost a baby too,' he said, his voice barely audible.

Zara's mind went into overdrive and her heart rate doubled. He'd lied to her? She'd asked him if he and Malinda had had children and he'd said no.

'You and Malinda had a baby?' she asked.

He shook his head quickly. 'No. I was married once, a long time ago. In my early twenties.' He dipped his head and quickly brushed away a stray tear before looking up and meeting her gaze again. 'You know that night I helped deliver Finn?' He stroked the back of his hands with her thumbs.

'As if I'll ever forget it.'

'Until that night I'd never delivered another baby.' He paused and looked up at her, tears running down his cheeks. 'Except my own. He was born sleeping.'

'Oh, Ryan. I'm so sorry.' She wished the stupid cast wasn't between them so she could get up and go to him to comfort him. Instead, she could do nothing except squeeze his hands and hope it was offering some measure of comfort. 'I'm so sorry,' she repeated. 'I can't imagine how painful that must have been.'

He brushed away another tear. 'Lisa, my wife, never knew. It was an emergency caesarean, and she lost a lot of blood. Her body went into shock and they couldn't save her. She died not knowing she had a son.'

Tears pricked her own eyes. She couldn't begin to comprehend how much he would have suffered. 'What did you name him?'

'William. After Lisa's dad who had died not long after we were married.' He swallowed. 'I buried my wife and son on the same day. It was the worst day of my life.'

Zara sat back and stared at him. How did someone get over something like that?

'I wish I knew what to say.'

He offered her a watery smile. 'There's nothing anyone can say to take away the pain. But the thing is, the night Finn was born mended part of the hurt.'

'And what happened today just tore you open again,' she concluded.

He nodded.

'Oh, honey, I'm so sorry. Whatever I can do to help, I'll do it.'

'Thank you.'

She waited for him to look up again then stared deep into his eyes. 'I love you, Ryan.' It was the first time she'd said the words and she wanted to be certain he knew she meant them.

A slow smile formed on his lips. 'I love you too, Zara. Lots and lots.'

Chapter Twenty-Four

The next morning Ryan helped Zara into his car, and they headed into town. The plan was he would drop her at the café and get the grocery shopping done, then they'd head to her parent's place to pick up Finn.

After placing her order, Zara stepped back outside into the sunshine and found a vacant table. She had just sat and rested her crutches against the wall of the café when she caught sight of Jodi Wallace. She groaned inwardly and debated whether to slip back inside, but Jodie had seen her and was heading towards her like a woman on a mission. Unable to hide or run, she leaned back in her chair and smiled in Jodie's direction.

'Hello, Zara.'

'Hi, Jodie. Good to see you again.'

Jodie's face was red, and her eyes were bright. And she looked like she had something to say. Zara suppressed a sigh. Who would it be about this time? She glanced back at the café, wishing

Georgie would hurry up with her order and come outside to rescue her.

'I thought you should know Dr Dunlop isn't who you think he is,' Jodie said when she got closer.

Zara lifted her chin. 'Is that right?'

'I'm sure you know about the stuff in Queensland. At the football club. The drug scandal.'

'I'm well aware of all of it.' Irritation pricked that Jodie—or anyone—was still trying to pull Ryan down over this. It was old news and Malinda had already admitted her role in the whole thing. 'There's no story there, Jodie, so don't go looking for something new.'

'I take it you don't know about the sexual assault charges then.' Jodie smirked and folded her arms over her ample chest.

Zara's stomach dropped to the ground, but she kept her face neutral. 'I beg your pardon?'

'I'm pretty sure you heard me.'

No, she couldn't be right. It wasn't possible. There was no way Ryan would have assaulted anyone. He was the gentlest man she'd ever met. He wouldn't hurt a fly.

'And when did this assault supposedly occur?' Zara asked coldly.

Jodie shifted from one leg to the other. 'Last year. It wasn't reported at the time, and no actual charges were laid, but it happened, Zara. It's all over social media and according to the woman he assaulted, it's only a matter of time before other women come forward and—'

'That's enough.' Zara lifted her hand, furious now, and it took all her self-control not to slap the smug sneer off Jodie's face. 'This type of small-town gossip is what ruins people's lives.'

Jodie tilted her head. 'I would have thought you, of all people, wouldn't stand by a man who sexually assaulted women. Wasn't that what you used to do? Fight for women in abusive relationships?'

'I don't listen to rumours.' Zara wished she could just get up and walk away.

Jodie shrugged. 'I'm trying to warn you, that's all. Ryan Dunlop is not the man you think he is and once the medical board hear the latest allegations, he'll be out of a job and out of town so fast you won't see him for dust.'

Zara glared at Jodie. 'You should be ashamed of yourself, trying to destroy an innocent man's reputation.' She clenched her jaw and forced herself not to say another word.

Jodie stepped back with a shrug. 'Fine. Whatever. Don't say I didn't tell you.'

Zara was trembling when Jodie left. By the time Georgie arrived with her coffee she was ready to explode.

'What was that all about?' Georgie asked with a frown in Jodie's direction.

'Nothing. Just Jodie being her usual self.'

'What? A bitch? She's trouble, Zars. Always has been. Whatever she had to say, don't believe a word of it.'

Georgie headed back inside, and Zara finished her coffee in record time. She needed to see Ryan and clear this up. As she headed for the supermarket to find him, anger at Jodie fuelled each step and Zara barely felt the discomfort of the crutches under her arms.

Her heart thumped against the wall of her chest. Deep in her gut she knew what Jodie had told her wasn't true. But now the seed had been planted and it dug at her conscience leaving her uneasy. Which was exactly what Jodie had wanted.

Ryan would clear this up.

*

Twenty minutes later, after she'd impatiently waited for Ryan to finish doing the groceries and load them into the boot of his car, they headed to her parent's house to pick up Finn.

From her peripheral vision, she felt Ryan's gaze burning into her. Around the corner from the pub, he pulled the car over, turned off the engine and swung in his seat to face her. 'What's wrong? You look like you're going to erupt. Have I done something to upset you?'

She considered saying nothing was wrong, but that wasn't who she was. She faced her problems head-on and didn't play games. Picking up Finn could wait. This conversation couldn't.

She sucked in a deep breath and exhaled slowly. 'Jodie Wallace just bailed me up at the café and told me you'd been accused of sexually assaulting a woman in Queensland last year. Apparently, it's all over social media.'

Dead silence met her question. His jaw was rigid, and his hands clenched the steering wheel.

'No. I have not. Ever. Assaulted. Anyone.' His voice was deceptively calm but firm as flint.

Relief swept through her. Of course, he hadn't. And yet Jodie said it was on Facebook. Someone was lying.

'Do you believe her?'

She swallowed hard. 'No. Of course not.' Although it seemed like a crazy thing for Jodie to fabricate. She wasn't that clever.

Ryan pulled out his phone and Zara remained silent while he checked it.

When he laughed, there was no humour in it. 'This kind of thing does my head in. Someone makes an allegation on social media and the gossip mill picks it up and carries it at warp speed.'

She bit her lip. He was right. She'd seen it happen before. Plenty of good men had had their reputations ruined by women in the same way women's lives had been destroyed by the men who'd promised to love them. All because of allegations, innuendo, and gossip.

'I swear to you on my life that I have *never* assaulted anyone, sexually or otherwise.'

She put a hand on his trembling forearm. 'I believe you, Ryan.'

He met her gaze. 'Do you? Because this kind of thing won't go away quickly or quietly.'

The solemnness in his eyes made her pulse race. 'I believe you.' She put her palm to his chest and felt his heart beating furiously against her soft touch. 'So, who is making this crap up? It's not just Jodie, is it.'

'My guess is Malinda.'

She searched his face for answers.

He gave a ragged sigh. 'My lawyer called yesterday but I didn't take her call. I was too busy with the baby and her mother. My guess is she was calling to give me a heads up.'

'What can I do?'

'I don't know. The problem is, if someone throws enough mud, it will eventually stick. There are still enough people who don't believe Malinda stitched me up with the drug thing.'

'We'll fight it together.'

'Thank you, Zara. You have no idea what your support means.'

'I trust you,' she said simply. 'Now let's pick up Finn and go home.'

*

After they arrived home and unpacked the groceries, Zara spent time playing with Finn while Ben made phone calls. Later, when Finn was taking a nap and Ryan was on his laptop having a Zoom meeting with his lawyer, Zara allowed herself to doze on the couch. When she heard someone pull up, she glanced out the window and saw it was Ben, in a police car. She frowned. He usually drove an unmarked car. Rather than get up to go to the front door, she waited, knowing he would let himself in.

When he did, his face was red, and his eyes were dark. 'Where's Ryan?' he asked, voice cold.

'In the spare room on a Zoom call.'

'I bet you haven't heard what he did.'

She exhaled loudly. 'Who told you? Jodie Wallace?'

'As a matter of fact, yes.'

'Ben. Come on. Are you going to believe Jodie or Ryan?'

'I'd like to talk to him.'

'Well, you can't. He's busy.' She awkwardly got up from the couch and with one crutch, hopped into the kitchen. Ben followed. 'Do you want a cup of tea?'

'Not especially.'

She flicked the switch on the kettle with more force than was needed. Taking out a glass from an overhead cupboard, she filled it with water from the tap and handed it to Ben.

He looked at her, lips thinned as he took the glass. 'Do you trust him?'

'With my life. And with Finn's,' she added. 'He's a good guy. Whatever he's been accused of, he didn't do it.'

'I don't want you or Finn to get hurt.'

She leaned back against the bench. 'I'm a big girl, Ben. I can look after myself. And I would never do anything that might jeopardise Finn's safety. The thing is, Ryan is amazing with Finn. We both know Finn is wary of people he doesn't know, yet he adores Ryan.'

His hands tightened around the glass. 'Zars, he allegedly assaulted his last girlfriend. How do I know he won't do it again?'

'First thing, he *allegedly* assaulted someone. She fabricated the whole thing. Secondly, give me a bit more credit for who I choose to spend my time with.'

Ben sighed. 'Do you love him?'

Emotion surged through her. 'Yes, I do,' she replied without hesitation. 'With all my heart.'

'What will happen when his contract ends?'

'He's already looking for something permanent.'

'So you won't leave Glengarrick and follow him back to Queensland?'

She shook her head. 'No. Not after the way everyone has helped me through my cancer and with Finn and now after this.' She tapped her leg. 'These people are my community. My family. I couldn't find that somewhere else. Ryan knows that. We talked about it right from the beginning of our relationship. Ryan knows Glengarrick is home.'

'And he's willing to make it his home too?'

'Very willing.'

Ben put his glass down and took her hands in his. 'I'm sorry. I shouldn't have barged in here accusing him.'

'No, you shouldn't.'

'It's just when I bumped into Jodie and she told me what he'd done, I just saw red.'

She squeezed his hands then released them. 'I get it. And I appreciate your concern. For me and for Finn.'

'I'm happy if you want to tell him about us. About Finn.'

'I will. When the time is right.'

Chapter Twenty-Five

Ryan stared, unblinking, at the screen in front of him. His first three patients of the day had cancelled. No doubt they'd heard Jodie Wallace's rumours. The waiting room was quiet, which was unusual for a Monday morning. Usually the phones were ringing with people making appointments after the weekend. If it wasn't for the people he could see walking up and down the street, he'd wonder if there'd been an apocalypse and he'd been left behind.

The morning session had run at a slower pace than normal and rather than the usual drop ins they got each day, there'd been none. Perhaps it would be best if he called the employment agency and let them know what had happened. That would give them time to find someone to replace him if they wanted to.

He exhaled slowly. Even if they replaced him, he wasn't going to leave. He couldn't walk out on Zara and Finn. Not now. The more he'd gotten to know them, the more he loved them.

He was just about to break his own promise not to check his social media accounts again when there was a knock on his door.

'Come in.'

Annie, the young receptionist who had started the same time he had, popped her head in. 'There's someone here to see you.'

At the worried expression on her face, tension coiled his muscles. 'Do you know who it is?' He glanced back at his screen. There were no more appointments until the afternoon session.

Annie nodded. 'He's not in uniform, but I recognise him. He's a cop.'

It would be Ben. Zara had told Ryan that Ben had dropped by the house on Saturday afternoon to express his concerns.

Annie nibbled her bottom lip and shifted from one foot to the other. 'What shall I tell him? I can't really say you have patients with you because it's like a morgue here today. I could say you've already left to go to lunch.'

'It's okay. Show him in.'

Moments later Ben stood in his doorway.

'Come on in.' Ryan pointed to a chair then closed the door behind Ben. 'What can I do for you? I presume you're not here for my medical expertise.'

Ben sat in the chair Ryan offered, took off his baseball cap and ran his hands through his hair. 'I'm not very good at this. I'm actually here to apologise.'

Ryan waited.

'I'm sorry for assuming the worst before I'd even spoken to you.'

'Just for the record, I didn't, and wouldn't, assault anyone.'

Ben nodded. 'Yeah. I know.'

'Surely you, of all people, would know rumours need to be verified before you go making accusations.'

'I was thinking like a friend, not a cop. I didn't want Zara to get hurt.'

'As her friend, you know she's a strong woman and more than capable of looking after herself.'

'Which is exactly what she told me.'

Ryan tented his fingers and looked at Ben. 'There's more to yours and Zara's relationship than friendship isn't there?'

Ever since he'd seen Ben and Finn together, he'd noticed the similarity between them. He had been surprised no-one else seemed to notice. Or if they did, no-one mentioned it.

'It's Finn, isn't it?' he asked.

Ben stared at Ryan, eyes wide. 'Did Zara tell you?'

'No. She didn't have to. Maybe because I'm an outsider, maybe it's because I'm a doctor. Who knows? But the first time I saw you and Finn together, it seemed obvious.' He paused. 'You're his father, aren't you?'

Ben exhaled slowly. 'I wish Zara had told you. I said she should tell you the truth.'

'Who else knows?'

'Annabel. My parents. Zara's parents. That's it.'

'I don't get why it's a big deal.'

'It's complicated.'

'Can't be that complicated. You and Zara had a baby. Question is, why are you both keeping it a secret?'

'You'll need to ask Zara. It's her story to tell.'

The phone on his desk rang and he glanced at it. 'I need to take this, sorry.'

'Zara's here to see you, Dr Dunlop,' Annie said.

Ryan glanced at his watch. Was it lunchtime already? Zara's dad had driven her to a doctor's appointment in Stockton and Ryan had arranged to have lunch with her afterwards before she headed back home.

He glanced at Ben and mouthed, 'It's Zara.'

Ben stood, but Ryan held up a hand asking him to stay. Perhaps the best thing would be for the three of them to talk things through.

'Thanks, Annie. Can you please ask Zara to come in?'

Moments later the door opened, and Zara hobbled in on her crutches, stopping when she saw Ben. She carefully took two steps back. 'I'm sorry, guys. I didn't mean to interrupt. Annie said to come straight in.' She looked from Ryan to Ben. 'I can come back later.'

'It's fine. He knows, Zazu,' Ben said.

She frowned. 'Knows what?'

'Ryan figured it out. He knows about Finn.'

Her shoulders slumped. She dragged her eyes from Ben and her gaze slowly met his. 'I'm sorry, Ryan. I was waiting for the right time to tell you.'

Ben edged towards the door. 'I'll leave you two to talk.' He put a hand on Zara's shoulder. 'You need to tell him everything.' He gave her a sharp look. '*Everything.*'

After he walked out, an awkward silence settled between them. Zara sank slowly into the chair Ben had just occupied, laying her crutches on the floor. While Ryan waited for her to say something, he fiddled with a pen, twisting it through his fingers. There'd never been this awkwardness between them, and he didn't like it.

When he realised she was waiting for him to say something first, he smiled, hoping it would ease the uncomfortable tension between them.

'Tell me what happened between you and Ben,' he said finally. 'Did you have a one-night stand then regret it?'

She screwed up her face. 'God, no. That would be like sleeping with my brother if I had one. Ben was my sperm donor.'

Ryan sat back in his seat and stared at her in surprise. That was the last thing he'd pictured. 'Sperm donor? Why did you need a sperm donor? Because of the cancer?'

She sighed softly. 'It's a long story.'

He made a show of staring at his watch. 'I have an empty waiting room and plenty of time. We can talk here now unless you want to go and get some lunch first.'

'Here's good. I don't want to be any place where someone might overhear us.'

'Are you hungry?'

'Not especially. You?'

'I can wait.'

She exhaled slowly. 'I guess I should start at the beginning and explain why I needed a sperm donor.'

'The beginning is a good place to start.'

'I used to be bisexual.'

He blinked twice. He had not seen that coming. 'Used to be?' he asked carefully.

'Long before I had Finn. I dated women and men, mostly women. That's why I asked Ben to be a sperm donor. I was with someone who I thought wanted to have a family with me. Turned out she didn't. It was all a bit of a disaster. Anyway, I figured I was turning thirty and I couldn't see how I was going to find someone to have a baby with me before my clock stopped.' She sighed heavily. 'I told you I had lots of baggage.'

'If you're worried whether I have an issue with your sexuality, I don't. As far as I'm concerned, fidelity is about being loyal to the person you love, regardless of their gender. But are you still...do you still think you're bi?'

She shook her head. 'Until I met you, I didn't know what it was like to be in love like this.'

He couldn't stand witnessing her heart break a second longer. He needed to comfort her and show her how deeply he cared. He got out of his chair, went around the desk, knelt beside her then took her into his arms.

'Oh, Zara, I love you so much. None of this changes that.'

He kissed the top of her head, her wet cheeks and forehead, then she buried her face in his chest.

She sniffed loudly. 'Are you sure?'

'We can work through anything. It's not a problem. Whatever happens, I am not letting you go. I'm in way too far over my head now. My life was set on a path with you the first time I laid eyes on you. That's just the way it is. It doesn't matter to me what you did or who you were in your past. What matters to me is who you are now.' He tilted her chin up. 'And I love the woman you are.'

'Thank you, Ryan.' She dried her tears with the back of her sleeve.

He sat in the chair next to her. 'Tell me what happened. You asked Ben to be a sperm donor?'

'Yes. And he took a lot of convincing, let me tell you. We decided we wouldn't tell anyone because we didn't think they'd understand, but then I got cancer and we knew we had to let a few people know. And then of course he met Annabel and it was important she knew from the start.'

'I wish you'd told me sooner.'

'I should have. I'm sorry.

'It's okay.' He stroked her back. 'Like I said, I had an inkling Finn was Ben's son when I first saw them together. I never considered sperm donation though. In some ways it makes it a bit easier than picturing you and Ben together, to be honest.'

She pulled a face. 'Ew. Like I said, Ben is like a brother.' She pulled out her phone, opened the photos app and found the album she'd created which had photos of Finn and Ben when he was a baby. She passed her phone to Ryan.

He scrolled through the photos and whistled softly. 'There's no way you were going to be able to keep this a secret for much longer.'

She took the phone back from him. 'I know.'

'What will you tell Finn when he's old enough to understand?'

'I always wanted to tell him the truth.'

'And Ben?'

'Initially he didn't want anyone to know, and he didn't want to be involved. We had a huge falling out and we didn't speak for most of my pregnancy. I only called Ben when I found out I had cancer. He's been by my said ever since.'

'He's a good man.'

'Are you sure it's not going to be an issue?' she asked. 'Ben is always going to be part of our lives.'

'Zara, we both have baggage. We both have our pasts, our histories. That's what makes us unique. What I'm more interested in is my future. My future with you.' He smiled. 'And our future together. If Ben's part of that, I'll deal with it too.'

*

After Zara left, he kept himself busy seeing patients for the rest of the day. His concerns that they might have been listening to Jodie's lies were unfounded. It turned out there had been a funeral that morning and his first three patients had cancelled to attend the service.

Just before six he was shutting down his computer and turning off the lights when his phone rang. It was Laura. She'd called and checked in with Ryan a few times since he'd taken over her practice, but he hadn't spoken to her since she'd had her baby.

'Hi Laura, congratulations are in order I hear.'

'Thank you.'

'Is it all going well?'

'Terrific. How about things with you? How are you finding the job?'

'It's great. Loving it.'

'I'm glad. That's why I'm calling.'

He heard something catch in her voice. 'What's up?'

'My husband has been offered a new job in Melbourne and we've talked about it and he's going to take it.'

Ryan's heart started to beat faster. 'So that means…'

'That means there's a clinic for sale if you want it.'

'Wow. You don't think you'll want to come back after your maternity leave? Even for a couple of days a week?'

'It would be too hard to commute from Melbourne. Nick has been offered a leadership role and to be honest, I'm already loving being a mum and can't see myself working full time again. We've already discussed having number two and given I'm nearly forty, I don't think we'll wait too long.'

There was a lot to process but Ryan's mind was already whirling with the implications of Laura's offer.

'You don't have to make a decision now,' she said, interrupting his thoughts. 'There's plenty of time to find someone to buy the practice but I'd really appreciate it if you could at least stay until the end of your contract.'

'I'll buy it.' The words were out of his mouth before he could stop them.

'Really? Do you want to have a think about it first? Talk it over with someone?'

'The only person I want to tell is Zara and she's going to be thrilled.'

Laura chuckled. 'I heard you two are serious. I'm glad this will work out for you.'

'More than you know.'

'Perfect. How about I draft a letter and email it through this afternoon. We can discuss details later.'

'Sounds good to me.'

Chapter Twenty-Six

Before heading home, Ryan stopped at the supermarket and picked up a bottle of champagne. He couldn't wait to share his exciting news with Zara. Even though there were a lot of hoops he'd need to jump through in order to purchase the practice from Laura, he had no doubt it could be done. Thankfully the figure she'd mentioned was more than reasonable.

His heart pounded every time he imagined the look on Zara's face when he told her the news. He'd continually told her he intended to stay in Glengarrick for good, but she often asked him how he'd planned to make that happen and he'd had nothing solid to offer her.

Zara opened the door before he had a chance to put his key in the lock and pressed against him, kissing him on the lips before sliding his jacket off his shoulders.

'That's a lovely welcome.' He held up the paper bag with the champagne in it. 'And I haven't even told you what we're celebrating.'

'Ooh, now I'm curious.'

She took the bottle from him and he followed her into the kitchen. The wood stove was burning cheerfully, and the house was toasty warm. Finn was in his highchair finishing a bowl of spaghetti, most of which was on the floor and down the front of his clothes. Ryan ruffled his hair. 'Hey, buddy. Have you been a good boy for Mum today?'

Finn nodded then went back to shoving the last of the noodles in his mouth and making more of a mess.

'You're going to need a bath before you go to bed,' he said with a chuckle. He turned to Zara. 'What smells so good?'

'Roast lamb.'

'Can I help with something? You're still not supposed to be putting too much weight on that leg.'

'I'm fine.' She poured him a glass of champagne and handed it to him before turning back to the stove. 'Dinner will be at least another half an hour. Do you mind bathing Finn for me?'

'Not at all.'

After he'd bathed Finn, Ryan got him into his pyjamas and encouraged him to get into bed. He was half propped up beside Finn reading him a story when Zara appeared. She leaned against the doorframe of Finn's room and watched them with a smile on her face.

He glanced up and smiled back.

'Dinner's nearly ready.'

'Do we have time to finish the story first?'

'Of course you do.' She walked into the room and leaned down to give Finn a hug and a kiss before leaving again.

As they ate dinner together, he smiled as she recounted stories of funny things Finn had done that afternoon. When there was a pause in the conversation, he set his glass on the table and dug out a piece of paper he'd stuffed in the shirt pocket under his jumper. It was a printout of the formal offer from Laura to buy the practice. He handed it to Zara.

'Here. Have a read.'

Zara's eyebrows arched as she took it. 'What's this?'

'You'll see.' He grinned, barely able to contain his excitement.

She unfolded the paper, and her eyes scanned the page before she looked up. Her mouth formed an O.

'Laura's offered you her practice?'

'Yes.'

'Are you going to buy it?'

He nodded.

'How did this come about?'

He explained Laura's phone call earlier that day.

'And you got it organised this quickly?'

'This is just a draft proposal. I haven't signed anything yet. Nothing's set in concrete, but yeah, I'm buying the clinic.' He smiled. 'If you know a good lawyer, I'm going to need one to look over the contract.' He scooted forwards and took her hands across the table. 'Zara, I want to spend the rest of my life with you.'

Her eyes widened and instead of the smile he'd expected, she pulled her hands out of his and twisted them in her lap. His stomach somersaulted.

'Zara?' He sat back and studied her face. 'What is it?'

'Ryan…the thing is, I want nothing more than to be with you for the rest of our lives…'

'But?'

He watched her swallow. 'I didn't mean to pressure you. If you don't want to get married, that's totally okay with me. I don't need a piece of paper to prove my love for you. I just want us to be together.'

She wiped her face before putting a hand up, asking for a moment. After composing herself again she said, 'this is a big step for both of us, and before we take it, there are some other things about me you need to know. I just hope I haven't left it too long to tell you.'

His stomach clenched. After she'd already divulged her history to him earlier, he didn't think she'd have much else to tell him. He sat back and stared at her, dreading that whatever it was she had to say might ruin everything they had together. No. He wasn't going to let it. Whatever else she wanted to tell him, they could work through it. He'd already promised her that earlier today and he meant it. This was a woman—and a relationship—he would fight for.

'I love you so much and this relationship is everything I've ever dreamed of and so much more. Our romance is perfect, and I love that you want to spend the rest of your life with me, I truly do. But what usually comes after marriage is kids.'

He frowned. 'Kids? You mean Finn. You know I love him, Zara. It doesn't matter that Ben is his biological father. I will love him like he's my own son. I already do. You know that.'

Her lower lip trembled, and tears welled up in her eyes, spilling down both cheeks. She hastily brushed them away with the back of her hand. 'The thing is, Ry, I can't have any more children. After the mastectomy they told me I was at high risk of ovarian cancer.' She started to cry, choking on her words. 'The advice was a full hysterectomy.' She turned slowly and met his gaze as more tears fell. 'I never had my eggs harvested or anything.'

Her words were a punch to the gut but the look on her face was pure agony. She was hurting more than he was.

'I'm so sorry, Zara.' He put an arm over her shoulders and pulled her close, kissing the top of her head. 'I'm so sorry. That must have been…I'm just so sorry.' He had no idea what else to say.

She gently pushed back against his chest and looked up at him. 'Do you understand what I just said? Do you know what this means? It means I can never give you a child of your own.'

She stared at him, waiting for him to say something, but he couldn't find the words. He rubbed his face with both hands before looking at her again. Unable to meet his eyes, she stood and excused herself for a minute to go and check on Finn, leaving him sitting there.

He couldn't believe it. Poor Zara. Not just the cancer and the surgeries, but to have the chance at having another child also taken away from her. It wasn't fair. To him, or to her. But what could he say? If he told her he didn't want kids anyway, that would be a lie. He'd always pictured having a couple of kids and, ever since falling for Zara, he'd secretly pictured them having a cute little girl that looked just like her and a son that, maybe, took after him.

Now that dream had been shattered and he wasn't sure how he felt about it. In the back of his mind, he knew they could probably adopt, but did they need to if they already had Finn? His mind was shot to pieces.

When Zara returned, he stood and held his arms open for her. On her crutches, she hobbled slowly towards him. He pulled her close and she neither of them said anything for a long time as she leaned her head against his chest. He pressed his chin gently on the top of her head. They'd find a way to make this work. They had to. He wasn't letting her walk out of his life now. Yes, it was true, he'd always wanted a child of his own, especially after losing William, but walking away from Zara because she couldn't have children with him was not an option.

Finally, she pulled back and looked up at him with red rimmed eyes. 'I totally understand if you want this to end, Ryan. It was selfish of me to let things get this far between us without telling you I couldn't have any more children. I hope you can forgive me. I won't hold any grudges against you if you want out. No one could blame you.'

He shook his head. 'I don't want out. God, Zars, I love you so much.' He took her hands in his and pleaded with his eyes, begging her to understand he was telling the truth. 'I might need a minute to process what you've just told me, but I'm not going anywhere. I just asked you to marry me, for goodness sake. And I'm not going back on that proposal.'

'But I can't have children. If you want a child of your own, I can't give you one.'

He put a finger to her lips. 'I hear you, Zara. And it's okay.'

She slipped from his grasp and hobbled back to the kitchen. He followed her, found her at the sink, her back to him, her body so tense he thought she might crumble.

He spoke softly, choosing each word carefully. 'I won't lie to you. I've always wanted children. Ever since William. But I want children with the right person. The thought of leaving you simply because you can't have babies is not an option for me. You have my whole heart. I don't want someone else. I want you. And Finn. I want the three of us to be the family I've always dreamed of.'

She turned around to face him, tears streaming down her cheeks. 'I hear what you're saying, but I think it would be best if you took some time to think about what I've told you. No matter what happens, I can't have any more children. God knows I've had plenty of time to think this through, but this is all news to you so…I don't know.' She shrugged. 'Maybe some space will be good so you can think it over before you make any decisions. You need to consider what your life will be like for you with a child who isn't biologically yours.'

He stared at her in disbelief. Space was one thing but why did it feel like she was breaking things off? The fact she was distancing herself from him hurt badly, mainly because he didn't know how to bring her back to him. All he wanted to do was fix what was broken and he didn't know how.

She wiped her cheeks. 'I don't want your life to be filled with regret. I don't want me and Finn to be your biggest mistake.'

'How is that even possible?'

By the look on her face it was clear he hadn't convinced her.

'I'll feel better if you come back to me fully understanding what you'd be giving up by choosing me and Finn. I can't be the reason you're unhappy because you don't have a child of your own. I can't live like that, always wondering if you regret your decision to choose me. I couldn't bear that.'

'I don't need time.'

She sighed. 'Yeah, but I do.'

He sucked in a deep breath. 'Okay.' But it was anything but okay. 'I will give you the space you need, and I promise while I'm gone I'll think about it, but let me assure you, my mind is already made up. I'm not walking away from you and Finn.'

She shook her head. 'I hear what you're saying, but you don't know how you're going to feel about the future because you haven't had time to think about it. And that's my fault. I should have told you sooner. Before it got this far.'

'Maybe you should have, but we're here now. Please don't shut me out, Zara. This is killing me.'

She dipped her head and when she eventually looked up, her eyes were clouded with guilt and sorrow.

'I just need to know you've taken time to think this through. If you come back to me, I'll know it's supposed to be.'

'Where do you want me to go?'

'Do you mind staying in one of the cottages tonight?'

Did he mind? Of course he minded.

Regardless, he went into the bedroom, his heart lodged in his throat as he silently threw some clothes and toiletries into a bag. How had his whole world tilted so sharply, so unexpectedly in less than an hour? It wasn't fair that she was cutting him off like this. It felt like she was punishing him because she felt guilty.

'I hate this,' he said as dropped the bag at the front door. 'I hate leaving things like this between us.'

'I'm sorry.'

'I know you think it's for the best, but surely it would be better for us to sit and talk about it. Give me a chance to fight for you. For us.'

'You're right but I can't explain it. I know you must think I'm being unreasonable—and part of me know that I am—but I just want you to have space to make your choice.'

'I've already made my choice. Going away for an hour or a night isn't going to change my mind.' He paused, Stared at her beautiful, tearstained face.

'Can I at least kiss you goodnight?'

She nodded and he kissed her tenderly, savouring every second of the connection before she broke away.

'I'm not going to stay away one second longer than I have to. When you're ready, I'll be waiting.' He pulled her tight and looked desperately into her eyes. 'I'll walk through fire for you. I will go from here to the other side of the world to be wherever you are. I want to be with you and grow old with you. I love you. And I love Finn. Remember that. Please.'

She was crying, but she kissed him softly before putting a hand on his chest and gently pushing him away. She nodded without speaking to show she understood.

His chest tightened as he walked out the front door and closed it softly behind him. Leaving her was like a slow tearing of Velcro. It was loud in his mind, pulling and scraping his heart strings the whole way.

As he walked down the hill to the cottage, his heart felt like it had been ripped from his chest. He loved Zara and she was going to have to work a lot harder to get rid of him if that's what she was trying to do. There wasn't another woman on the planet like her and there was no way he was letting her slip through his hands.

Chapter Twenty-Seven

An hour later Georgie walked into Zara's house without knocking. Ryan must have called her. Zara was on the couch under a blanket, surrounded by a pile of used tissues, where she'd been since Ryan had gone. She was bone weary and didn't even have the energy to get up and stoke the fire.

'He called you, didn't he?' Zara asked, looking up blearily at Georgie.

'He called Jed. He didn't have my number.' She opened the door to the fire and threw in some logs. 'It's freezing in here.' Once the fire was going again, she went into the kitchen. Zara heard her tidying up then she came back a few minutes later with two mugs of steaming tea.

'Tea fixes everything.' Georgie handed a mug to Zara.

'What did Ryan tell you guys.'

'Not much.' She pointed to Zara's glass of untouched champagne. 'What were you guys celebrating?'

'Laura wants to sell the practice to Ryan.'

Georgie's eyebrows shot up. 'That's great news isn't it?'

Zara nodded.

'Then why are you crying and why isn't Ryan here?

'Because I'm an idiot.'

'No, you're not, honey.' Georgie brought her tea to her lips and blew on it.

'You'll think so when I tell you what I did.'

'Whatever happened, we can easily figure this out. I'm not letting you push him away. He's perfect for you and you're so good together.'

'I told him everything. As in *everything*, George. About me being bi. About Ben being Finn's father. The fact I can't have any more kids. I dumped the lot of it on him.'

Georgie carefully put her mug down on the coffee table. 'How did he take the news about Ben?'

'Good. Great. Better than I could have hoped. He'd pretty much joined the dots anyway. He said it's obvious Finn looks like Ben.'

'Yeah, I have to say, the older he gets, the resemblance is clear.' She took a sip of her tea and swallowed. 'What about when you said you can't have any more children?'

'Shocked, I guess. But he was kind and caring and considerate and wonderful.' Zara buried her face in a couch cushion. 'Exactly how you'd expect from a guy as sweet as Ryan.'

'I'm still confused about why you told him you need space.'

'I don't need space. He does.'

Georgie frowned. 'Did he tell you that?'

Zara shook her head. 'I want him to have time and space to think about a future that might not include children of his own. I insisted he take time to decide how he truly feels about me and Finn and everything I told him about. I need him to be one hundred percent certain he knows what he's getting. I need a partner who won't look at me some time down the track like I've trapped him in some life he didn't choose. I love him too much to let that happen.' She looked Georgie directly in the eyes. 'He asked me to marry him.'

Georgie's eyebrows shot up. 'He what?'

'He didn't get down on one knee, but yeah, he said he wanted to spend his life with me.' Zara hugged the cushion to her chest. 'I'm an idiot, George. The guy proposed, and I rejected him. Tell me I didn't just make the biggest mistake of my life.'

Georgie looked at her. 'I wish I could say you did the right thing, but if I were in walking in your shoes, I wouldn't have pushed him away. I would have found a way to talk and work this through together.'

'What if I have too much baggage and he can't handle it?'

'Zara, you need to listen to me right now. It's time you took a good look at yourself. You have the strength of forged steel. From my earliest memories of you in high school you were the brave one, the one with all the crazy ideas. The strong one. Sure, some things in your life haven't gone the way you might have planned, but all things have worked out for good in the long run. Whether you turned to the left or the right, things always sorted themselves out.'

Zara chewed on a thumbnail. Georgie was right. Even though life had battered and bruised her, things always seemed to work out.

Georgie reached for hand and squeezed it. 'Yeah, the universe dealt you a tough blow with the breast cancer. I can't imagine what it's like to lose your breasts and lose your chance to have more children, but you're a fighter, Zars. And this is just one more fight I know you're going to win. But please don't fight *against* Ryan. Stand with him and fight your fears together. Two are better than one and if he's half the man he seems to be, he's not going to let you walk away.'

Tears welled in Zara's eyes and her throat closed over. 'What if he thinks I have too many problems and he doesn't want me?'

'I think you're underestimating him. A bit of baggage isn't going to scare him off. Besides, it would be weird if women of our age didn't carry some form of baggage, don't you think? All it means is, you've lived life well through all its craziness. You are resilient, Zara. You've already proven that. Choosing to have Finn on your own. Fighting and beating cancer. It's your strength that Ryan finds attractive.'

'I guess so.'

'Of course, he does.'

'But I still think he needs time to process it all.'

'Like I said, work through this together, not apart.'

'I should call him.'

'In my opinion, yes. But ultimately that decision is yours to make. But whatever you choose to do, and whatever Ryan chooses, I know you will be okay. And you'll always have me and Ben and all your friends.'

She leaned forward and hugged Zara tightly.

'Thank you, George. I couldn't have done the last couple of years without you guys.'

'The last word I'm going to say is this: Ryan isn't your enemy. You need to stop pushing him away because you're trying to protect yourself from being hurt. There's no guarantee in life we won't be hurt. You already know that. But if you're going to get knocked down again, wouldn't it be better knowing you have someone like Ryan in your corner ready to pick you back up? You already admitted you love him, so do yourself the biggest favour of your life and let him love you back.'

Chapter Twenty-Eight

The weight of Zara's confession pressed down onto Ryan like a dark cloud. His chest ached as he lay in his bed at the cottage that night, staring at the ceiling. His thoughts whirled loudly, making it nearly impossible to sleep. When he finally did, he was plagued by nightmares of drowning, reaching out to Zara who was being swept away from him in a strong current. He kept trying to grasp her hands, but she wasn't looking at him and didn't see he was so close.

The next day at work it was hard to concentrate on his patients. His mind was so full of thoughts of Zara he found himself apologising more than once for not hearing what someone had said. It killed him that he and Zara had got themselves into this place in their relationship and yet neither of them had done anything to create a fight or a problem. Until last night, he'd thought everything was going smoothly. Now it felt like they were breaking up and he was powerless to stop it happening.

As he'd told her last night, there was nothing more to discuss as far as he was concerned. He'd already made up his mind. He could let go of this fantasy about having a son who looked and acted like him or having a daughter who was just like Zara. He could walk away from all of that and build a new dream as long as it was with Zara. They could do it together if she let him.

He somehow got through the day, but rather than go straight back to the farm, and the empty cottage, he stayed at the clinic doing paperwork. Laura had already sent through a contract for the sale of the practice—he was surprised how quickly she'd had it drawn up—and he wanted to look over it before he showed it to his lawyer and discussed it with the bank. It was only when his stomach growled and realised it was pitch black outside that he checked his watch. It was after eight o'clock.

He sighed. It was so easy to slip into old habits. When he was with Malinda, if they'd had an argument, he used to avoid her by staying at work. He didn't want to repeat those patterns with Zara. He wanted to face things head on and talk. But how was he supposed to do that if she pushed him away?

He knew for certain he was in love with Zara. He knew he never wanted to be without her. But he also knew that deep down he'd planned on having a family of his own. Children of his own. He'd hoped that would be with Zara, never for a moment imagining that she couldn't have any more children. When she'd told him, she'd beaten the breast cancer, he'd never thought to ask if it had affected any other organs and as a doctor, he should have considered that was a real possibility

Now, having children of his own wasn't an option. Was he okay with that? Could he imagine life with just Finn? How would he deal with knowing Ben was Finn's biological father and still very much on the scene? At least Ben seemed like a great bloke and he could imagine their friendship deepening, but the question was still there.

He shut down his computer and turned off the lights. After locking up the clinic he got into his car and drove slowly down the main street. The pizza shop was already closed, as was the Thai takeaway. He didn't want to get a meal at the pub and risk running into Zara's parents, which left the Indian restaurant.

After ordering enough food for dinner that night and a week of leftovers, he stopped at the bottle shop next door to the pub and picked up a six pack of beer. He wasn't usually a drinker, but tonight it seemed like a good idea to have at least one.

As he waited for his dinner, he stared mindlessly at the television without really watching. His mind was on Zara and their situation. He wished he were with her, sitting at her dining table by the window in her kitchen, eating take-away Indian curries with her. Instead, he was about to head back to his cottage, alone. He picked up his phone and stared at it, wondering if he should call her. She hadn't said how much time and space she needed. Surely twenty-four hours was long enough.

As he was getting into his car, his hands full of take away food containers, his phone buzzed with a text message. The second he saw it was from Zara, his heart leapt in his chest. He put the food on the passenger seat and read her message.

How are you doing? Hope you had a good day. I can't stop thinking of how much pain I've caused you and I'm sorry. Just want you to know that no matter what you decide, I love you.

There was no way he was texting back. Pulse bounding, he called her. She answered on the first ring.

'Hey.' Her voice was soft, and he pictured her nibbling her bottom lip.

'Hey, you. How are you doing?' he asked.

'I'm okay.'

'Yeah, well I'm not. I can't do this Zara. I can't go home and sit less than a hundred metres from you and think about everything you want me to think on my own. I want to be with you talking it through face to face. This isn't your problem alone, Zara. It's ours. And it's not even a problem. It's just something we need to figure out together.'

'I know.'

'Please, don't shut me out and pull away from me. I know you think on some level that you're doing me this great favour by giving me time to decide, but it's killing me,' he said, hearing the catch in his voice. 'I've already made my decision and I've told you I love you and I want to be with you.

'It's killing me too,' she said softly.

He could hear her tears through the phone, and it tore at his heart.

'Oh, honey. I don't want a life without you in it. We've both already lost so much. Let's not lose each other too. I want to be with you, whether we are married or not. I want a family with you, whether that's just Finn and us or whether we decide to adopt or foster. Whatever our family looks like, I'm okay with it.'

'Oh, Ry.'

'I'll never love anyone the way I love you, Zara Pritchard.'

'I love you too.'

'Can I come home?'

'Please do.'

'I'm on my way.'

When they hung up, Ryan let his head fall back against the headrest and stared out through the front windscreen as rain began to fall. He'd never felt happier in his entire life. As he drove down the darkened road out of Glengarrick towards Zara, Ryan smiled for the first time that day. He felt like he'd run a marathon, but slowly the tightness in his chest was easing. They'd would work this thing out.

The light rain soon became a downpour, and his wipers had a hard time sluicing away the sheets of rain pummelling the windscreen. He slowed down, straining to see in the dark. A car overtook him, and he swore loudly when it swerved back in front of him, nearly cutting him off before tearing off into the distance. Seconds later, he could barely make out its taillights up ahead through the driving rain.

'Idiot.'

The glow of headlights coming towards him sent halos of fragmented light all around and he slowed further. The two-way road was narrow enough as it was. Once the car had passed him, he flicked his high beams on, but they did nothing to cut through the rain. The wipers made a thudding sound as they arced across the glass. He saw a flash of red taillights and started to brake. Even though he was only going sixty, his car felt like it was aquaplaning.

Moments later he passed a car pulled off to the side of the road at an odd angle. He pulled up fifty metres in front of it and stopped as far off the road as he could without being in the ditch.

He switched off his engine but left his headlights and hazard lights on. Stepping out of the car he was instantly soaked. He cautiously approached the car. As he drew closer, he saw the shredded back left tyre. A young woman was standing in the rain staring at it.

'Are you hurt?' Ryan asked.

She shook her head. 'I'm fine. But I have no idea how to fix this.'

'Pop the boot and I'll give you a hand.'

'Maybe I should just call roadside assistance.'

'They'll take hours. I can fix it now and you'll be in your way in no time. I hope you have a spare.'

She nodded as she leaned in and pressed the button for the boot. 'It's Dad's car. He takes good care of it. Maybe I could call him.'

'I'm happy to help.'

'Only if it's not too much trouble.'

He desperately wanted to get home to Zara, but another half an hour wasn't going to matter.

'That wasn't you speeding past me earlier, was it?'

'No. Someone tore past me too. I think that's how I punctured the tyre. I went off the side of the road.'

Ryan lifted the spare from the boot and was reaching for the jack when he turned and was blinded by the headlights of an oncoming car. There was no time to move.

His last thoughts were of Zara and Finn and how much he loved them both.

*

Eyelids heavy, Ryan felt like he was floating. When he opened his eyes, Lisa was standing at the foot of the bed. She wore her wedding dress and her hair hung down loose around her shoulders. Her smile warmed his heart. He hadn't dreamed of her in years.

'How are you doing, Ry?'

'Not so good.'

'You'll be fine. Zara is a wonderful woman, and she needs you to keep fighting, okay?'

'Oh, Lise, I didn't go looking for someone to replace you.'

'I know. Zara came into your life when you didn't realise you needed her. Finn did too.'

'He will never replace William either.'

'He's never supposed to.'

'What if she won't let me love her?'

'She will. She'll realise she's blessed to have you. Just as I was blessed.' Lisa smiled. 'You deserve to be happy again, Ry.'

The light behind her seemed to grow brighter, illuminating her hair and shoulders. Ryan's heart beat faster, and he had the sense this was the last time he was going to see her.

'Lise, don't go yet. I need you.'

'It's okay, you have Zara now.'

Even though he still felt Lisa's presence, the light had swallowed her up and she was gone.

Chapter Twenty-Nine

An hour after she'd spoken to Ryan, there was no sign of him. She was trying not to be worried, but something wasn't right. She'd called his number three times and each time it had gone straight to voicemail. As she picked it up to try again, it rang.

Ben. Her heart sped and the air left her lungs. Ben would only call if it were bad news.

'Zars, there's been an accident.'

'Is it Ryan?'

'Yeah.'

Her blood pounded in her ears and even though Ben was talking, she couldn't hear what he was saying. She felt like she was about to pass out. Panic rose in her chest and the room spun. She forced her breathing to slow.

'You there, Zara? Annabel's on her way to come and look after Finn.'

'Wh…what…what's happened?'

'He was driving home in the rain and there was an accident on the road. He stopped to help and was hit by another car. The driver didn't see him in the dark and the rain.'

There was silence on the other end for what seemed like an eternity. Her mouth was dry.

'Is he alive?' she asked finally.

'Yes, but he's not in good shape. The retrieval team is on their way and they're going to airlift him to Melbourne. You need to get there. That's why Annabel's coming over. You sort things out with her, and I'll swing past and pick you up in half an hour and drive you down to Melbourne. Pack clothes. You'll probably want to stay in a hotel for a few days at least.'

'I can't lose him,' she said.

'You have to think positively.'

After hanging up, she reached for her crutches and pulled herself to her feet, cursing her broken leg for hindering her speed. She was stuffing things into a suitcase when she saw headlights coming down the drive. She hobbled through the house to open the door and accepted Annabel's warm hug.

'He's going to be alright, Zara.'

'He has to be,' she said as a sob escaped her lips.

'Are you sure you're okay with me looking after Finn? We just thought it was better than ringing your parents and asking them to drive out in the rain.'

'Of course. Yes. Absolutely. As long as you don't mind.'

'To be honest, looking after Finn might keep my mind off my morning sickness.'

'Are you okay?'

'Totally fine. Don't worry about me.'

'If he's too much, just call Mum in the morning.'

'Of course. Now, can I help you pack?'

Zara pointed to her bag. 'I don't even know what I've thrown in there.'

'Go and get dressed and I'll make sure you have everything you need.'

Zara glanced down and realised she was in her pyjamas. 'Thanks, Annabel. I really appreciate this.'

'You'd do the same for me in a heartbeat.' She smiled at Zara. 'That's what friends do.'

While she would have loved a shower to wake her up, it took too long to slip her cast into the plastic bag she used for showering. Instead, she splashed water over her face and sprayed deodorant and cleaned her teeth. By the time she was dressed and ready, Ben was pulling up out the front. The rain had stopped but the ground was covered in muddy puddles. Putting her crutches in one hand, she hopped across the veranda and let Ben help her down the steps and into his car.

'Call me when you have news,' Annabel said, standing at the door, backlit by the lights inside.

'We will.'

Zara wound down her window. 'Please pray,' she said, starting to cry again.

Annabel waved and smiled sadly. 'I've already started.'

*

Dawn was breaking on the horizon when Ben and Zara arrived at the hospital in Melbourne. Once again, she cursed her broken leg for slowing her down as she relied on Ben to help her through the carpark and the maze of corridors to the emergency department. He'd offered to get her a wheelchair, but she wouldn't hear of it.

At the reception desk, she let Ben take the lead. If necessary, he'd pull out his badge and get answers more quickly than she would.

'Excuse me, we're looking for a patient called Ryan Dunlop. He was airlifted here from Glengarrick earlier this morning.'

The woman behind the Perspex screen looked at her monitor and her fingers tapped the keys on her keyboard. Zara felt like she was going to vomit. She finally looked back to them. 'He's in surgery. Head to level five and check in with the ward clerk. She'll show you to the waiting room.'

Ten minutes later the two of them sat side by side in a waiting room and the dreaded clock-watching began. The ward clerk had already warned them it could be hours before there was any news. The longer Zara sat, the more anxiety built within her until the urge to scream sat just below her throat, lingering in her chest wall. Her mind refused to think of anything except worst case scenarios.

She must have dozed off on Ben's shoulder because she jerked awake when the door opened and a woman in scrubs and a bright coloured cap entered the room. Outside, the sun was up.

'Are you Zara Pritchard, Ryan Dunlop's partner?'

'Yes,' she managed, getting to her feet with Ben's help.

'I'm Sarah Elliot. One of the orthopaedic surgeons.'

Ben stepped forward and shook the doctor's hand. 'And I'm Ben. Zara's friend and one of the first on the scene. I'm a cop, but I was off duty.'

'Please, take a seat.' Sarah motioned to the chairs behind them. 'What did you do to your leg?' she asked, pointing to Zara's cast.

'Broken in three places. Horse riding accident six weeks ago.'

Sarah smiled. 'You and Ryan will be able to compare notes then. He's broken the same leg.'

'He's okay then?' Ben asked.

'He will be. He has a long recovery ahead of him, but I think he will be fine. Ryan was flown here after sustaining serious injuries when he was hit by a car. The good news is the ambulance crew got to him quickly and said he was semi-conscious for a few minutes on the scene and, despite pain, had full movement in all his limbs.' Sarah glanced at Zara when she exhaled heavily. 'When he arrived, he was in bad shape, mostly because the paramedics found it hard to get on top of his pain. Scans showed a fractured shoulder and leg, broken ribs and a punctured lung. His back is fine and it's a miracle none of his internal organs were damaged.'

'What about head injury?' Zara asked.

'We're monitoring his brain function. He took a blow when he hit the ground, but so far the swelling isn't too significant.'

Zara exhaled again as relief washed over her.

'He's not out of the woods but he's young. He's fit and he's strong. And right now, he's in ICU in a coma, so I suggest you guys find a hotel and get some sleep. Keep your phone on and one of the nurses will call you when they lighten sedation later this afternoon.'

'Thanks, Sarah,' Ben said.

She stood and smiled tiredly at them. 'I'm off to get some sleep.'

'You deserve it. Thank you and the rest of the team for everything you did,' Zara said, also standing.

'Just hold tight and if you're praying people, that's the best thing you can do.'

Once Sarah was gone and the door closed behind her, Ben held his arms open, and Zara fell into them and let the tears stream down her face.

'He's going to be okay, Zars,' he said, stroking her back. 'Be strong, think positive thoughts.'

'I wish I could see him,' she said, through sobs.

'You will, but not right now. Let them do what they need to do and let's do what the surgeon said. We both need sleep.'

'To be honest, I'd prefer a coffee.'

'So would I.'

Chapter Thirty

The soft sound of insistent beeping filled Ryan's ears. At first, he wondered if he was still dreaming. He forced one eye, then the other to open, even though it felt like he was pushing back against the weight of steel gates. As his vision slowly began to focus, he realised he was in the hospital.

The accident.

He felt himself starting to panic and the beeping on the monitor accelerated. He was intubated and couldn't move his right shoulder or left leg. Was he paralysed?

A woman in scrubs—nurse or doctor, it was hard to tell—wearing a plastic apron appeared at his side seconds later.

'Hello. Nice of you to wake up. I'm Beck,' she said cheerfully.

He tried to bring his left hand up to point to the tube, but it was weighed down with something and every tiny movement brought excruciating pain to his rib cage.

'Don't try to move too much. You've got an arterial line in your left arm and your right shoulder is in an immobiliser sling. We've been lightening your sedation all afternoon, but you clearly needed a good sleep. Once you're a bit more awake, we'll pull the tube, okay? And then I'll fill you in on what we've been up to while you've been having a slumber.'

He blinked once and gave a tiny nod.

'I know it's hard, but just try to relax. Are you in any pain?'

He nodded again.

'Rightio. I'll be back in a second.'

While he waited for Beck to return, he glanced around the room as much as he could. Even though his left leg felt heavy, he could wiggle the toes on both feet, which was reassuring. Not paralysed.

Beck returned with a man by her side.

'G'day, Ryan. I'm Reynold, the ICU consultant.'

Ryan blinked. This man didn't look old enough to be out of school uniform.

Reynold chuckled. 'I know, I have a baby face. Trust me though, I am a doctor.'

'A good one,' Beck said as she laid a bluey across Ryan's chest and got out a syringe and an oxygen mask. 'I think he's alert enough to pull the tube.'

'I agree,' Reynold said. 'Can you lift your head off the pillow a bit?'

Ryan did, but it made him cough.

'You'll feel a tug and it will be all over. Beck will put some oxygen on, so don't try to talk straight away. Just give yourself a few minutes to steady your breathing.'

Beck swiftly pulled the tube, and despite his sore throat, it was instant relief. Ryan let his head fall back against the pillow and closed his eyes as she slipped the oxygen mask over his face.

'Good job, Ryan. Doing well.'

'What happened?' he asked a few minutes later, his voice hoarse.

'Do you remember anything?'

He nodded.

'You were hit by a car when you were changing a tyre on the side of the road.'

He frowned. He'd seen Lisa. Or was it Zara? His brain felt muddled.

'The good news is you're going to be fine and make a full recovery, but it will take time. You have three broken ribs and a punctured lung. The pain in your chest is from the chest drain. Hopefully that can come out in the next day or so.'

'I can't feel my leg.'

'Broken. It's in an immobiliser, as is your arm.'

'Internal injuries?'

'No. Remarkably. You'll be bruised and sore, but you are one lucky man. We were a bit concerned about your head, which is why you were intubated, but the CT's are reassuring. No bleeds on the brain.'

'What time is it?' Ryan asked. He didn't even know what day it was.

'Four o'clock in the afternoon. And it's Saturday.'

He closed his eyes and tried to visualise his calendar. 'Zara. I need to tell Zara.'

'She's outside in the waiting room,' Beck said. 'I called her a couple of hours ago to let her know you were waking up. As soon as I have you cleaned up a bit more, I'll bring her in to see you, okay?'

He winced, partly from pain and partly from worrying about Zara. She was here though. That had to be a good thing didn't it?

'Only short visits though. You need to rest. Clear?'

'Crystal,' he said with a small smile.

*

It was half an hour before Beck decided he looked okay, and the room was tidy enough to allow visitors. He heard Zara before he saw her, grumbling about how much her crutches were slowing her down. He had to smile. Between them they weren't going to have enough good legs for a three-legged race.

The moment she entered the room he knew they were going to be okay.

The frown on her face disappeared the second she saw him and, even though he still had wires and tubes coming out of everywhere, she managed to find a way to gently hug him.

'Oh Ryan, you have no idea how worried we've all been.' She brushed a strand of hair away from his eyes as tears pooled in hers.

She blinked them back.

'Don't cry, honey. It's okay. I'm okay. It's going to be alright. I'm going to be fine. I'll be back on a horse in no time.' He lifted his good arm. 'Come here.' She took his hand and squeezed his fingers.

'I just didn't know…even though the surgeon said you were okay you were taking so long to wake up and…we weren't sure…I was so worried you'd hit your head and maybe you'd forgotten me…I was so scared.'

'I haven't forgotten you at all.'

'But do you remember what happened just before the accident?'

'Yeah, I do. We were talking about spending the rest of our lives together, weren't we?'

Her mouth dropped open. 'You still want me? Even after I pushed you away?'

'I want you more than words.'

She kissed him gently on the cheek. 'I love you so much.'

'I love you too.'

He closed his eyes, inhaled and exhaled. When he opened his eyes, she was still there. He wasn't dreaming.

Zara stroked his arm. 'I don't know what I would have done if…' she began.

Ryan squeezed her hand. 'Don't go there.'

She leaned over and kissed him softly on his lips. 'I love you, Ryan Dunlop.'

'I love you more.'

Epilogue

It was a stunning December day with blue skies and not a cloud in sight. Zara was busy supervising her friends who were helping her decorate her parents' pub for tomorrow's big day. A white marquee tent had been set up out the back in the beer garden, complete with a dance floor. Over the road from the pub in the community garden, a white arbour had been set up and her mum had covered it in roses of all different shades. White timber chairs with pink ribbons were set out in a semi-circle facing the arbour, which would serve as the focal point where she and Ryan would make their vows.

Jed was helping Georgie carry large potted plants and flowers from his ute and they were placing them around the dance floor. Ben and Annabel were helping too, but Annabel was inside with her feet up, working on table decorations. Their baby wasn't due for six weeks, but she'd had a difficult pregnancy and was taking it easy. Ben watched her like a hawk.

Zara smiled as she gazed around the pub. It looked better than she'd expected. When her parents had suggested Zara and Ryan have their simple wedding at the pub, she'd never pictured it like this. But with Georgie's catering and flair for decorating, plus hours spent on Pinterest, it had come together perfectly.

After Ryan's accident, his physical recovery had been slow, but they hadn't altered their plans to get married. When he was still in ICU in Melbourne, he'd joked that as soon as he could go down on one knee, he was going to propose. It took ten weeks of intensive rehab and physiotherapy, but he was true to his word. Now, less than two months later, they were about to have the simple wedding they'd talked about.

Life was working out perfectly. The sale of the practice had gone through seamlessly, and as well as working at the clinic, he was helping Zara run the B&B while also project managing the new extension and renovations to the main house. In between all that, he somehow found time to help Jed with pre-season training down at the footy club and exercise the horses with Zara. She was still planning to go ahead with her equine therapy program, but that had been put on hold for a bit longer. Even though her leg had fully healed, her confidence had taken a hit and she hadn't been back in the saddle since her accident. Ryan kept reminding her it was okay to take things slowly.

'Is everyone okay if I head off?' Zara asked. She still had lots to do at home to get ready for the big day, including a special surprise for Ryan and the bridal party.

'We're fine, darling,' Mum said. 'What about you? Do you need anything?'

'I'm all good.'

More than good. A year ago, Zara couldn't imagine her life looking the way it did right now. Still battling the emotional scars of her cancer, she never imagined she could be in the place she was in today. And she certainly never imagined she'd be able to fall in love and trust someone the way she loved and trusted Ryan.

She'd felt like damaged goods after her cancer—empty inside—until Ryan walked into her life. Even though she had Finn and the gift of motherhood and incredible family and friends, something had been missing. Someone to share her life with.

The best part was she was in love with a man who loved her in return. And even better, he adored Finn and Finn adored him. Because of Ryan, they were both stronger, happier people. He'd brought her back to the person she was before cancer, continually promising that together they would face life's challenges head on. They would lean on each other for strength and embrace every second of life, knowing how fragile life could be.

She was in the stables finishing off the last touches on Colby when the horse's head snapped up and his ears pricked. She turned around to see Ryan standing there.

'What are you up to?' he asked, a slow smile spreading across his face. 'Why are you plaiting your horse's mane? I would have thought you'd be inside getting yourself ready for tomorrow.'

'Ah, sprung,' she said with a laugh. 'This was supposed to be my little secret.'

Ryan stroked Colby's blaze. 'Plaiting Colby? I don't understand.'

'I'm going to ride him down the aisle tomorrow.'

A frown creased Ryan's brow. 'In your wedding dress?'

She nodded. 'Yeah. We've been practising, haven't we Colbs?' She patted the horse's neck. 'I was worried he might freak out if I tried to get on him wearing a big white tent of a dress, so I've been getting on him wrapped in a bedsheet. He couldn't care less.'

Ryan chuckled. 'Oh, honey, I'm sorry to spoil your special surprise.'

'That's okay. You can act like you knew nothing. Anyway, it'll still be a surprise for everyone else. Only Dad knows because he's going to lead Colby and walk beside me and help me dismount.'

'It will be perfect.' He took her hand and folded his fingers over hers. 'Just like you.'

She smiled. 'And wait until you see Finn in his little suit. He's adorable. I just hope he doesn't muck up and throw a tantrum.'

'Where is he now?'

'At Ben's.' She glanced up at him. Even though Ryan seemed to have to issues that Ben was woven into the fabric of their lives, she was always careful to check that it wasn't an issue. 'I hope that's okay. Ben wanted to get him ready for tomorrow.'

'Of course it's okay. It's probably important for Ben to do this.'

'I think so. I had a long chat to Annabel the other day and she said Ben felt like this was his chance to hand Finn over to your care, if that makes sense.'

'I think it does.'

'A bit like the old-fashioned way of my dad giving me away to you. Ben wants Finn to know that you're his dad now.'

Ryan's face took on a distant look.

Zara cupped his cheek with her hand, sensing where his thoughts had gone. 'William will always be a part of you,' she said softly. 'As will Lisa. I promise I won't let their memory fade.'

He looked down at her. 'How do you do that?'

'Do what?'

'Always know what I'm thinking?'

She pressed her lips against his. 'Because I know you.'

'Do you know how much I love you Zara Pritchard?'

She grinned. 'You may have told me once or twice, so yes, I have a fair idea.'

'Then I reckon we should go and get married, what do you say?'

'I say yes.'

If you enjoyed this book, please click below for the other books in the series:

Off the Field Series (Small town Romance)
Book #1: The Final Siren

Book #2: Settle the Score

Book #3: The Last Quarter

Acknowledgements

Writing can be an incredibly solitary job. Most times it doesn't worry me because I'm quite happy with my own company. But this book couldn't have been written without a little village of helpers to cheer me on, I would like to indulge and take a moment to acknowledge these people.

Firstly, I want to thank and recognise my friend Delwyn Jenkins. You couldn't find someone the polar opposite to me in so many ways, yet I would drop everything for her in an instant, just as I know she would do the same for me. Which is precisely what happened with this book.

2020 was a difficult year for everyone, but as we turned the corner into 2021, I realised my life was about to become even more chaotic with the rollout of the Covid19 vaccination through GP clinics, which is where I work. In addition to working four days a week, I am still a wife and a busy mum of four adult kids.

To fill our already full lives we decided we'd finish the renovations on our house ready to put it on the market. Plus, I am now riding and competing on Monty, so my attention is pulled in so many different directions. In the background was the constant stress of knowing I had a book that just wouldn't write itself and it played on me day and night.

In sheer desperation I reached out to a few of my gorgeous author friends: Delwyn, Lisa Ireland, Alli Sinclair and Andrea Grigg, and through tears, told them how worried I was about this book. I honestly had no idea how I could complete it, even after extending the deadline by a month.

Bless her heart, Delwyn stepped in and offered to do a full structural edit and Andrea did the copy edits in a twenty-four-hour turnaround. My gorgeous daughter Chloe also dropped everything to proofread the final version with literally hours before it needed to be uploaded. Their excellent help saved me, and this book. Without them I would have had to admit defeat.

I also want to thank authors Belinda Williams for her support, encouragement and brilliant blurb writing, Joanne Tracey for providing me with photos of Sunshine Coast sunrises that kept me going when our skies in Geelong were dreary and grey and matched my mood, Annie Seaton for fabulous cover design and Susanne Bellamy for some initial editing of the first draft.

From the bottom of my heart, I thank each of my author friends for rallying around me and showing how much you care. I hope one day I can return the favour or pay it forward.

So, dear readers, if there were any minor mistakes—some typos or slips of grammar or some inconsistencies in the storyline—I ask your grace and forgiveness. It was either that, or not finish the book and I didn't want to let you down.

In case this is the last book I write (I'm not saying it will be, but I definitely need to take a break), I want to acknowledge my amazing husband. Without Tim grounding me, I have no idea where I'd be. We are hopefully entering a new season in our lives in the next six months and for that I couldn't be more excited. For anyone who has read my bio, you would have read the following paragraph:

"Nicki's dream is to one day escape to the country and live on land surrounded by horses, dogs, cows and sheep. Unfortunately, until that happens, Nicki will continue to live vicariously through the lives of the characters in the books she loves to read and write."

Well, hopefully our dream is going to come true very soon. Right now, we are busy searching for the perfect property so Monty and I (and all the other animals I'm hoping to add to our menagerie) can have our own country town escape. As always, I'm sure to share the journey on social media.

Finally, thank you to you, the readers, who have come along for the ride. When I woke up one day at the start of 2014 and said, "I'm going to write a book", I never dreamed I would have fourteen published titles six years later. It's because Haylee Nash (who was at the time the editor at Momentum then Pan Macmillan) took a chance on me as did you lovely readers. I sincerely hope there are many more books in my future, but I won't promise anything for now. It's "see you later", not "goodbye".

Take care. Much love,

Nicki

PS. Please stay in touch. I love to read your reviews and love it when you share how much you've enjoyed one of my stories.

Also by Nicki Edwards

Escape to the Country Series (Medical Romance)

Book #1: Intensive Care

Book #2: Emergency Response

Novella: Operation White Christmas

Book #3: Life Support

Book #4: Critical Condition

Novella: Operation Mistletoe Magic

The Peppercorn Project

One More Song

Holding Onto Hope

Second Chance Christmas

Novella: Lake of Dreams

About the Author

Nicki is a city girl with a country heart. Growing up on acreage outside Geelong in Victoria, Australia, Nicki spent her formative years riding horses, hand rearing lambs and pretending the neighbour's farm was her own. After spending three years in a regional town in New South Wales in her twenties, Nicki's love of country towns and rural life was further developed.

Nicki's dream is to one day escape to the country and live on land surrounded by horses, dogs, cows and sheep. Until that happens, Nicki will continue to live vicariously through the lives of the characters in the books she loves to read and write.

A voracious reader, Nicki always wanted to be an author. After returning to university as a mature aged student to study nursing, Nicki juggled full time study, part time work and raising four small children to achieve her dream of becoming a nurse. But her other dream—the dream to write—never left, and in January 2015 Nicki had her first book published.

Nicki now divides her time between writing, working as a nurse in General Practice or riding her retired racehorse Monty (race name Moderator).

Nicki and her husband Tim have four young adult children, two spoiled border collies (#mollyandindie) and an ancient Burmese cat called Roxy.

To stay up to date with her latest releases, please visit Nicki's website: http://www.nickiedwardsauthor.com/ or find her on Facebook or Instagram where she spends far too much time!

www.ingramcontent.com/pod-product-compliance
Lightning Source LLC
Chambersburg PA
CBHW010516100726
47903CB00009B/2767